SPECIMEN

SPECIMEN

Personal Essays

MADISON HAMILL

Victoria University of Wellington Press

Victoria University of Wellington Press
PO Box 600, Wellington
New Zealand
vup.wgtn.ac.nz

A catalogue record is available from the
National Library of New Zealand.

ISBN 9781776563012

Published with the assistance of a grant from

Printed by 1010 Printing International, China

Contents

The New Leadership

When I was ten, turning eleven, and until I finished primary-intermediate school, I had a teacher named Lance Woods. Like the lancewood plant, Lance Woods, or Mr Woods as we knew him, always had his eyes on the heights to which his pupils would one day ascend. Up there, in ghost form, were all the great leaders of history: Nelson Mandela, Ghandi, Harriet Tubman, Winston Churchill, Martin Luther King Jr, Kate Sheppard, Ed Hillary. It didn't matter what they fought for, particularly. Mr Woods wasn't a Christian, a Buddhist, an activist or a pacifist. What mattered was that these leaders had character, and character was made of values. Long lists of these values were written on thick marigold-coloured paper and pinned to the walls of our classroom. Initiative, Responsibility, Respect, Diligence, Loyalty, Helpfulness, Humility, Caring, Determination, Duty, Honesty ... It was

Mr Woods's mission to shape us from the lazy, disrespectful good-for-the-dole kids that we could have been into young leaders. Through hard work and determination, we would embody so many of these values that strangers would meet us and be inspired, and think to themselves, 'That young person should be prime minister one day.'

Once, I asked Mr Woods what humility meant. 'Well, that's easy,' he said. 'It's just thinking about others, as well as yourself, isn't it?'

We'd always had Road Patrol badges, or it may have been that there had always been Road Patrol but nobody had thought to offer badges for it until Mr Woods came along. Road Patrol is the task of wearing an orange jacket and pushing out the orange lollipop to stop traffic at the zebra crossings outside the school.

Then he introduced the SAFE badges. SAFE stood for Safe and Friendly Environment. On SAFE duty, we were required to patrol the junior playgrounds, sorting out disputes, telling younger kids to wear sunhats and shoes, watching out for accidents, making sure no one was hogging the play equipment. Everyone in our class had a turn at SAFE duty, so it was no big deal, but to the juniors, we became akin to teachers—powerful, able to recommend them for detention or writing lines. They would find us in the playground and say 'So and so pushed so and so', and we would mediate.

Most of us liked being in charge, though there were some complaints at first. 'Aren't we just doing the teachers' jobs for yous?' one boy asked Mr Woods.

'Do you want to be a wee kid?' said Mr Woods. 'Some people say you're just children and can't be trusted. But I know better. You're young men and women now, and I think you can handle a bit of responsibility, don't you?' As he said this, he was holding his hairy legs wide apart, jiggling one leg up and down and spinning a baseball bat around in his palm. Despite all this, we listened to every word he said. We were so used to being told we were just kids who couldn't be trusted that we felt a surge of righteousness. We could be in charge. We weren't babies anymore.

Once SAFE was established, he brought out the PAL badges: Physical Activity Leaders. On PAL duty, we were in charge of starting a game at lunchtime—setting up the equipment, rallying people to play the game, and then supervising. Everyone was a PAL in our class, but we had to wear a green badge the size of a business card at all times. We liked the way our badges took up space on our uniforms and made us stand out from the younger kids.

Then came the silver leader badges and the gold leader badges. We were observed for how well we exhibited leadership values, how well we did our PAL and SAFE and Road Patrol duties, and how well we did our homework. The best were rewarded with silver leaders' badges, and, if they maintained their record and somehow showed themselves to be even greater at still more of the listed leadership values, they would become a gold leader.

We wanted those badges as if they would make us famous and make our parents love us. Mr Woods was a fun guy. Even I, who was not fun and so did not have fun with him, believed that he was fun, as if it were an objective value independent of my experiences. He would take us out for PE every afternoon for the greater part of the day so we could play non-stop cricket on the big field. I could never keep track of the ball. For me, cricket was like watching the screensaver with the ball that bounces off the sides of the screen. But I was the odd one out in my opinions on sports.

Maths with Mr Woods was game after game of speed times tables. The whole class sat in a circle and a multiplication question was yelled at you and if you didn't answer quickly enough then you were sent to the bottom of the circle.

Once, we learned the one thing I was good at: story-writing. Mr Woods's advice was 'twists and turns, kids, lots of twists and lots of turns'. He and his favourite student, Holly, wrote a story together in which every sentence had a lion or a sword fight or a freak accident or a magical resurrection. He read it aloud to the class, laughing. My own story had only one twist and no turns. It was about the seagulls outside the window. 'Ours is the best,' said Mr Woods. 'Best story ever written. You can't argue with that.'

Every morning when the first bell rang, Mr Woods gave a speech. These speeches got longer and more involved over time. We would gather around him as he praised those among us who were cultivating leadership values, and told stories about people overcoming obstacles and stepping up. 'When I was a bit older than you guys,' he said, 'I was doing very well in footy, but I had a bit of an anger problem. When anyone did something I didn't like, I would lash out. But I had a coach who believed in me. He made me the team captain, and he said, "Lance, if you keep behaving like this, you're going to go down a bad path. But I know you can do better. You have what it takes to be a leader." And he gave me a list of leadership values, the same as I have given you, and he said, "This is what a leader

10

looks like. I need you to show me you can step up." And I did. The next time one of my teammates said something to set me off, I stopped myself, and I thought, What would a leader do? And when I started doing this, I noticed my teammates started listening to me and respecting me. And that's how I became the leader I am today.'

Even though I knew there was something not quite right about the leadership system, I wanted to be a leader so badly I prayed to God to make me a better person. I also prayed to Allah and to any other gods out there, just in case my parents were wrong on the religion front. I did my homework, researching the great leaders of history all afternoon and printing and cutting out pictures of Nelson Mandela to paste into my homework book. I tried to be kind. I gave money secretly to charity, tidied the classroom, opened doors for teachers, did my SAFE, PAL and Road Patrol duties to the best of my abilities, and tried hard in class. But the people who got the badges were the ones who were not just loyal, respectful and initiative-taking, but also talkative and good at sports, and they liked to fetch Mr Woods's coffee (six cups a day) from the staffroom unprompted during class-time. I was not extroverted. I rarely spoke in more than one-word sentences.

'Good morning, Madison,' Mr Woods would say when I came into the classroom.

'Morning,' I would say, looking at my shoes. Somehow my voice was never loud enough to reach the range of human hearing. I would psych myself up before school each morning, saying to myself, 'You're going to say "Good morning, Mr Woods" in a loud voice, and smile, and make eye contact.' But when the moment came I would forget everything.

One afternoon, as everyone was leaving, Mr Woods took me aside. 'Maddy,' he said, 'don't you think it's rude not to answer in more than one word when someone asks you a question? Do you think that's gold leader behaviour?'

'No,' I said.

'Oh, for heaven's sake,' he said.

A few days later he gave us conversation lessons. We practised having adult conversations, answering each question in full sentences and offering a new question in return.

When gold leader badgers had become more common and attention started to drift, Mr Woods invented the prefect badges. They were gold and shiny and had a big capital letter P on the front. Prefects were the coolest of the cool. When you were deemed a potential candidate, a letter was sent home to your parents so that they could report on your behaviour at home. 'You can't just be a leader at school,' Mr Woods said, 'you have to be a leader every second of every minute of every day.' He wrote this in capital letters underneath the lists of leadership values.

I had one friend named Rachel. Rachel was good at being a leader. She joked along with Mr Woods and made friends with his favourites. She was also the smartest in our class. She always did the best homework and loved learning about the great leaders of history and the Seven Wonders of the World. She wasn't good at sports like the top leaders were, but one day there was an event about young leaders, and all the local schools went. There were sort-of famous people there from TV who gave motivational speeches, inspiring us to be the leaders of the future, and at the end of the night there was a leadership award for kids who'd been nominated by their teachers. Rachel won. From then on, she became a favourite. Rachel had thought that when my short story about a drought in Africa won an award from the newspaper that Mr Woods would like me too and we could be leaders together, but he barely mentioned it. Rachel spent more and more time trailing the leaders. I walked up and down corridors trying to look like I was going somewhere.

Mr Woods introduced the chicken game. In the chicken game, everyone had to stay in one third of the netball court, and one person was given a rubber chicken. Their job was to whack someone with the rubber chicken as hard as they could. Extra glory could be won by leaving a mark. Then the person who had been hit would have the rubber chicken. When a few girls complained about the violence, Mr Woods said that to show he wasn't being unfair, he would join in. When Mr Woods had the rubber chicken, you had to run fast. He had been a professional soccer player in his day. One boy was left with a chicken-shaped bruise on his arm from where Mr Woods had hit him, and he showed it off proudly. A group of us once tried to avoid playing and stayed inside typing a letter of complaint to the principal about the game. When we were called out to play, we got scared that we would get detention, and gave up. Later, one other girl and I finished the letter and posted it anonymously into the suggestion box in the school office.

A few of the prefects were chosen for a free ride in a helicopter after the St John Ambulance team visited to show us their equipment. The rest of us watched them from the ground.

Anyone who acted out had their badges removed and

started losing friends. One of these kids was a boy named Nikau. He lived in a council house near the dog park. He had a good sense of humour and a speedy athletic frame, so he should have been popular, but he was stripped of his badges after getting into a fight. When a girl named Kate started dating Nikau, Mr Woods brought them both to the front of the class and told them to break up. 'Repeat after me,' he said, 'I hereby break up with you . . .' Kate cried and repeated the words, while Nikau stood sullenly and said nothing. Then Mr Woods had the class sing the Blue's Clues song 'Mail Time'. 'Here's the mail, it never fails. It makes me want to wag my tail. When it comes I want to wail. Mail!' And he presented Nikau with a detention slip.

I hated Mr Woods, but I still believed in the values of the leadership system. I believed in Diligence, Caring, Initiative, Humility, Duty. Any dream of resistance centred on showing Mr Woods that I embodied these values. And yet, I hated him, and I wasn't the only one. Parents were writing letters of complaint to the principal, my own included. There were mutterings of unfairness among the class.

One day, Mr Woods said that our class was to organise a fundraiser for our school camp. All the senior classes would bring money to school to spend on games that our class would organise. 'Any ideas?' he asked us, brandishing a whiteboard marker.

'Cream pie the teachers,' someone suggested.

The class became hysterical.

'All right,' said Mr Woods, 'I'm game. I can take a few cream pies.'

On fundraiser day we lined up with paper plates full of

14

budget shaving cream (real cream was too expensive). In turn, each of us threw a plate at Mr Woods. He grinned as I launched my paper plate with my full strength, shouting, 'Ha,' and instead of the satisfying hard splat I was hoping for, it flew, light as a paper plane, and slid gently off his chest.

'You can do better than that,' he said, grinning. I felt silly. What had I been expecting? Nothing could hurt him or humiliate him. He may as well have thrown a cream pie at himself.

When we finally went on our class camp, my dad volunteered as parent help. He saw how I trailed mutely behind the other kids, like an understudy. 'You must have been so miserable,' he said. I felt ashamed.

Eventually, almost everyone in the class gained their silver badge, and the majority their gold badge. The badges clinked together when we walked, dragging our shirts down, the metal pins like scales against our chests. Somehow, I was working my way up the ranks. One day, after months of perfect behaviour, I was doing an activity in another class with a nice teacher named Mrs S, and when she asked me how my day was, I answered in two full sentences. Mrs S reported this back to Mr Woods, and a letter was sent home to my parents to confirm my perfect behaviour. I became a prefect. I still didn't have friends, but once a silver leader girl sat next to me on the bus to ask for advice. 'How did you do it?' she asked. 'How did you become a leader while being so shy?' She wanted to read my homework book to figure out the secret.

'I don't know,' I said. 'I just tried really hard and then I improved.'

Years later, I tried to turn my time with Mr Woods into a

novel. The main character was a version of me named Marnie. I gave Kate's break-up story to Marnie. But I also gave Marnie a secret escape. At lunchtimes, Marnie would go into a secret hollow part of the hedge. She could sit in there, while the kids screaming and renegotiating their leadership status on the bright field outside looked like stars in a great green night. In the hedge she met a boy who had stumbled in by accident and they shared the secret place and became friends. Of course, in real life my secret hollow was a toilet cubicle and my friend was busy sucking up to Mr Woods. In this way, I made Marnie's life both better and worse. By removing some of her loneliness but giving her Kate's public humiliation, I was making Marnie more like the heroes of real novels. Harry Potter, for example, never dreaded getting up and going to school in the morning. He was rescued by a giant with a pink umbrella and sent to a magical school where his differences belonged and had a purpose. In a sense, Harry was saved from loneliness as a precursor to saving the world. Harry Potter faced public threats and public humiliation. Inside, he always knew his worth. Depression did not exist in his world, except in its physical manifestation, the Dementor, a ghostly hooded creature which floated invisibly through the world, sucking good feelings out of people and sucking out their souls. Except wizards can see Dementors. Harry Potter is saved from a Muggle's life of dealing with things you can't see.

I made Marnie more like him because I didn't know how else to tell my story.

One day, Mr Woods took me aside and handed me a detention slip, my very first. My heart pounded. 'You know what this is for, don't you?' he said.

'No.'

'It's rude,' he said, and I realised I had answered in one word again. 'You can go sit in detention and take some time to think about how you're behaving.'

I took the little red slip of paper to the office. The secretary looked at me in surprise, and I felt my face burn. She directed me to a small room behind the office, where there was an old wooden desk with swear words scratched into it. I stared out the window and hoped no one would come down the hall and see me. I didn't understand why I was there. If it wasn't something I'd done, it had to be something I was.

The week after that, Mr Woods called the class together and said, 'You know, this leadership thing is voluntary. It's your choice to be a leader. It's a choice you make every single second of every single minute of every single day, and if any one of you wants to give up, and give back all your badges, you can do so. Just hand them back, no explanation needed.' I don't know why he said that. Perhaps there were too many parents complaining and he wanted to prove he wasn't forcing us to do anything. Perhaps he genuinely wanted to offer a way out for those of us who weren't happy. But we were used to his speeches, and we knew the implication—if we gave up our badges, we weren't leaders. It wasn't just our roles we would be giving up, but our values.

At the end of the day, when everyone else had left, my friend Rachel and I stood in the corner of the class, whispering. 'I can't give mine back,' she said. 'You know I can't. I've got a reputation. I need them to like me. But if you want to, you should do it. I'll support you.' She walked out of the room and waited for me outside. I took my badges off my shirt one by one, except for the PAL, SAFE and Road Patrol ones. I kept those to show that I wasn't lazy. I took off the prefect and silver and gold badges and I walked over and handed them to Mr Woods.

'I guess not everyone is leadership material,' he said.

I've thought, since then, about what I could have said in response. I considered what Marnie could say. She could say, 'I don't need badges to be a leader.' Or she could say, 'I guess not,' and look him dead in the eye. But I made her say nothing, as I had done, and it was okay—Marnie was still the heroine. I didn't need to overcome my quietness. I didn't need to change Mr Woods's mind in order to change my own.

When I walked away, the badges no longer clinked together on my chest. I felt the way a pigeon might feel if it were to claw its way out of a medieval pie before its cue. I felt powerful.

Suspending Belief

When I was nine, I played Christmas carols on my flute outside the mall to capitalise on the Christmas spirit. I needed money to buy more Barbie accessories. I had hopes that my Barbies would one day live in a world created just for them.

I'd chosen the flute because it had the purest sound. I'd listened to all the string, brass and woodwind instruments and concluded that the flute was objectively the best one because it was the least compromised by textural buzz. Later, in high school, I would change my mind and begin to hate the sound, as I associated it with innocence and angels, but by then it was too late; I was already good at it.

My mum dropped me in an entranceway with my equipment and left to do some shopping. Christmas shoppers rustled past, talking loudly to be heard over one another. The cars growled fume-ily at the crossings and music from the nearby doorways overlapped uneasily—Avril Lavigne and 'Jingle Bells'.

I hated the beginning of a busking session the most. I hated setting up, with the knowledge that, just by being there with my angel wings and my equipment, I'd made myself a stage and plonked it unsolicited in the middle of other people's business. I had to make a show of getting out my flute, setting up the music stand, clipping the carol book to the stand with pegs and adjusting my angel wings, all business-like, to assert my legitimacy as a busker.

I especially hated playing the first note. In the shopping mall, a flute sounded like someone had broken into the pet shop and released an exotic songbird, and I was the burglar swinging open the cage door. It took a few lines of 'Away in a Manger' to feel that I'd established my sound as part of the Christmas cacophony.

I had just begun to play the last song in the carol book, 'We Wish You a Merry Christmas', when a woman stumbled into my peripheral vision. She moved unsteadily and smelled strongly of alcohol, but she was smiling. She had on a Santa hat and was banging on a tambourine. I knew her immediately. Everyone who considered themselves a true local in our city knew her by her first and last name, but no one knew her well enough to use just her first name, so she was always her name in full, and we were prideful in our knowledge of her name, acting as though she were a friend we saw from time to time but never spoke to. In *our* city, we believed, we only really had one homeless person, and we knew her name, and she wasn't even really homeless, since she actually had a council house and a team of therapists.

She came up beside me and began to sing along, loudly and in one long slur that only vaguely resembled the tune. I looked around desperately as I ploughed on through the second verse. I wished my mum would come back. Passersby were beginning to take longer glances in my direction. I didn't want to seem rude, so the pair of us continued with 'We all want some figgy pudding, we all want some figgy pudding' and 'We won't go until we get some, we won't go until we get some'—though she wasn't singing the lyrics identifiably. I hated this song to begin with, not just because it was so repetitive, but because it was about carol singers demanding 'figgy pudding'. I assumed this was Christmas pudding and I hated Christmas pudding. Hearing it made me taste it in my head, and the word figgy tasted exactly like those green and red glacé cherries in their fibrous, spicy cake mush. Now the rhythm was being warped by the singing in my ear, and the smell of alcohol swamped me every time I took a breath. I became so trapped by the thought of what the onlookers must think, perhaps believing that I had volunteered myself to this, that I was a terrible, tone-deaf musician, and most of all that I hung out with *her*.

Finally, I spotted my mum in the doorway of the nearby shop. I tried to call for help with my eyes. It's difficult to do when playing the flute, since flute-playing lends itself naturally to expressions of surprise, so it just looked like I was reaching for a high note. Mum was looking at the woman. She frowned and cocked her head to the side slightly. Then she came up beside her and started singing too. She looked the woman in the eye as she took command with her assertive Sunday School soprano.

'Why?' I moaned afterwards. 'Why did you do that to me?'

I'd cast this woman as my enemy and all I could see was that my own mother had assisted in my debasement.

She shrugged. 'I thought it might help her find the tune.'

My parents love their enemies. This is a defiance of the eye-for-an-eye mentality of the Old Testament and of meritocratic capitalism. Luckily, they don't have real enemies, so while in my imagination this principle involves standing in front of guns aimed at dictators, their lives don't involve many guns or dictators, so they content themselves with being nice to call-centre operators and offering back-up support to street performers.

Once I had a job interview for a call-centre role at an insurance company. I was put in a conference room with other applicants, and we were told that there were ten people in a failing elevator and we only had time to save seven of them. Luckily, we would have enough time to decide which of the people to save and which to allow to plummet to their deaths. Information about the ten people's characteristics, roles and economic worth were provided for our perusal. I suggested we ask for volunteers from the ten people on the elevator, but it was explained to me that each of the people in the elevator wanted to be saved and would not volunteer to be left behind. Each person was standing equidistant from the door, waiting cooperatively to be saved or not saved as their rescuers decided, neither offering to pay for their own salvation nor volunteering to be sacrificed, nor curled in the foetal position paralysed by anxiety, unintentionally making it difficult for themselves to be saved.

There were a variety of people in the elevator. One was young and wealthy and had many people's jobs under his control, but he was also arrogant and kept his wealth to himself. Another was an active and loved member of the community but also a great-grandfather nearing the end of his natural life. There was a good plumber bloke, a young mother, and a genius who was a bit of an arsehole but had just discovered the cure for cancer. I wondered which system for ranking the value of human life would make me more suitable to provide advice about insurance.

We agreed to kill the billionaire and the old man. I did not get the job. I asked what it had all been about and they said that it hadn't mattered which people we chose to save. It had all been a trick to see how we worked collaboratively—how we decided as a team the value of the ten lives, and how we respected each person's point of view. Presumably, then, it was the person asking for the perspectives of those who kept quiet, the one who was most enthusiastic in encouraging participation in the choice-making or who was most prepared to compromise their position for the sake of team cohesion, who got the job in the end.

I asked my parents what they would have done, and they said, 'How horrible and bizarre.' They said it was an artificial situation, since nobody should be in the position of deciding whose life is of more value than another's. I tried to explain that if you didn't decide, all ten characters would plummet to their deaths, but they refused to participate. I thought they probably would not make good call-centre insurance providers.

*

When I was much younger, my mum could break an apple in half with her bare hands. She did handstands and swam in hailstorms and regularly pulled out all the hairs on her legs with a device called an epilator. My dad rollerbladed to church in his ministerial robes and knew about what happened to people after they died. My life was full of superheroes. David shot Goliath and Moses parted the sea in two with his bare hands like my mother breaking an apple.

At some point, I developed an elaborate picture of what 'normal' parents were, based on my friends' parents and parents from TV. Then my parents became embarrassing, clueless and bumbling. The powers they once seemed to possess became trivial in comparison with their many abnormalities. My mum wore a fanny pack and yodelled in public when she could not find us in the mall. She took bunches of black bananas out of rubbish bins in waiting rooms full of other parents and loudly announced her plans for banana cake. In many ways, Dad was the more normal parent. If he hadn't been a church minister, he could even have been a cool parent.

The Sunday School teachers told me that David shot Goliath, the giant, with his slingshot because he was very brave. When they told the story, they tried to imply that Goliath was just stunned for a little while, that he might have gotten back up and wandered moodily back to giant land, regretting his mistake. But everyone knew Goliath was dead. The teachers also told me that Noah made a boat and filled it with two of every animal and then God murdered everyone else on earth and all of the excess animals. Then God made a rainbow because he regretted killing all those people, and he told everyone to love their enemies. I thought it was probably just a way to mask his guilt.

When I was ten, a cheerful man came to our school and

explained that God had saved us all from our sins by allowing his son to be publicly executed. The man was very happy about this, but most people in the class were confused as they hadn't known what sin was or that they needed to be saved from it. Luckily, I knew all the answers because I'd been to church. I put my hand up and answered all the questions. A lot of people had questions that they didn't ask, because they didn't want to seem interested in Bible in Schools. I sensed that a lot of people were thinking, 'How can he love us unconditionally and then expect us to follow a set of commandments?'

Yes, that is a contradiction, I said in my head as I answered the questions of the people who had asked them in their heads, *but there's an explanation*. I couldn't remember what it was, though. I had a terrible anxiety as I struggled to answer the questions my classmates hadn't asked, and I could see how they must presume that the people on the main street handing out scare-pamphlets about Hell were representative of Christianity, and it made me angry that the cheerful man was allowed to teach it all wrong. I still put my hand up to explain about what happened at Easter, though.

Morality weighed greatly on my mind when I was eleven. In my diary I cut out pictures of celebrities from *Creme* magazine and glued them into the categories 'good' and 'evil'. Paris Hilton was evil, and Anne Hathaway was good. On my bookshelf was a collection of stories called *Women Who Made a Difference*. Most of the women were the wives of missionaries. One was a mother who spent all her free time praying for her son to become a Christian, and then he did become a Christian and then she died happy. The women in the book were all very good, mostly because they didn't get upset about having to live boring lives and pray a lot. Once they were good Christians, they didn't want things like Barbie accessories and they ate plain, healthy food and translated the Bible forever. I wasn't much like the women in the book. Sometimes when my sisters did something annoying, I'd feel a disproportionate rage, as if the world was a big trap, and I'd claw at my sisters' arms with my fingernails.

Around that time, my brain became a vast TV streaming service. I could choose any channel I liked and pick up a story where I'd left off, inventing it as I went along. I imagined extravagantly. I imagined being forced to play piano for Voldemort's dinner party where everyone was dressed in Gothic clothes and suppressing their humanity out of fear. I imagined chase scenes across vast landscapes and witty exchanges with my favourite villains. When my parents took me to classical music concerts, I used them as soundtracks for violent prison breaks. When I went to church, the meditative atmosphere was perfect for impressing my enemies with my wit and fearlessness, and for rescuing attractive princes from their outdated world views. All of my enemies were in love with me, but I wasn't in love with them.

I returned to the real world when required, and it was like being woken up roughly. I had to smile and say hello to people. I had to go to school and pretend to enjoy it and worry about who was looking at me and where to sit. I felt tired; I wanted to return to the stories in my head.

When I thought about it from the perspective of an omniscient being who cared about my moral health, I saw that my thoughts were selfish and inward-looking. When I was present, I was always seeking to protect myself by worrying about what others were thinking about me, which distracted from what they were saying. Naturally, I imagined what God must think of me. Even if you know God is not human and cannot be imagined, if you suspect there is an omniscient, omnipotent presence watching you, then you have to imagine what they see. I felt guilty about how I'd behaved towards my sisters, not just about a single incident but multiple, building up, and even though each particular incident had been resolved, some larger summation of these events didn't feel resolved. I knew that it wasn't as simple as having your virtues weighed against your sins when you died. Dying didn't seem like a real problem. It was just that I felt I'd gone bad inside and I needed to do something.

I took all of the gold coins out of my piggy bank. It wasn't much, but gold coins felt valuable to me, being the heaviest kind of money. I put a handful in each pocket. My sisters and my parents were all in the living room. I could hear my sisters fighting over the cake batter. I went first to my older sister's room. I found her piggy bank on the desk, dropped one pile of gold coins, wincing as each one crashed onto the cash inside, and then I left, my heart thumping in my ear.

I listened in the hall. There were still chairs moving and voices. My younger sister's room was trickier because the money box was in the wardrobe. I strained my ears as I walked. I could still hear them, but I sped up anyway. I found the box, a pirate treasure box, made mostly of tape and paint. I had to unclasp it at the front to open it. I grabbed the coins from my pocket, shoved them in and closed the box again.

'Were you stealing from my piggy bank?' I had put it back and stepped away when she appeared. I had been so intent on imagining her in the living room, my blood leaped.

'No, why would I steal from you?' I said.

'I saw you touch it,' she said, forcefully.

'I was just looking for the dress-up jewellery,' I said.

I felt clean afterwards, like I really had fixed something.

I reached my peak religiosity at Easter camp when I was twelve. Easter camp was a camp for Christian teens on Easter weekend. It involved lots of normal camp stuff, like team sports and obstacle courses and campfires, with the added elements of bible discussion groups, feeling sombre about Jesus's execution, and daily singing of contemporary worship music while waving one hand in the air to feel the Holy Spirit.

My friend Rachel wasn't Christian, but when I invited her she came. In bible discussion groups she made up stories about feeling close to Jesus.

'So this is where all the hot guys are,' Rachel whispered as we sat around the bonfire on Easter night. 'Who knew? They're all at Jesus camp!'

I hadn't noticed it before then, but she was right. There were a lot of hot guys at Easter camp. A lot of them were in Christian folk bands. I felt a strange pride in knowing that I had inherited an ideology endorsed by hot people.

I tried putting one hand in the air during the singing, and it worked. There was a song about being washed clean by the Holy Spirit and I could feel the Holy Spirit detoxifying me from my hand all the way into my gut. I could see that this Holy Spirit thing was a sort of drug. You could feel yourself being forgiven; it was a pure feeling, just like how I'd felt after putting the money in my sisters' piggy banks.

One day I would sort out the questions I had about some

of the biblical details like the angels and virgin births and heaven. I was given the impression that it was an all or nothing situation. At some point, you took 'a leap of faith', and when you reached the other side of the leap, all of that made sense too. But I wasn't sure that wanting to feel pure was a good enough reason to make that leap without first straightening out the logistics.

My dad organised an introductory Christian course for youth when I was about fourteen. We learned that some of the events in the bible had really happened and some were just parables or stories to illustrate a point, and some were from before Jesus came along, so that was more of a prologue anyway. Many things were hard to understand because they'd been written by multiple people over hundreds of years, or because the target audience was 2000-year-old middle-eastern Jewish labourers, or because the translations were ambiguous. For instance, 'eternal punishment' could be translated as 'the chastisement of the age to come', which was not eternal but a kind of temporary restoration process. At the end of the course, each of us could choose if we wanted to make a leap and officially confirm our faith in front of the congregation.

'Maddy, do you want to do it?' my dad asked. 'You don't have to.'

I sighed and rolled my eyes. 'What's the point? It's just a ceremony.' What I really thought was, *Maybe I'm just not capable of belief.*

I hoped that my lack of belief was a phase I would get over one day, but I was no longer sure, and anyway, I was suspicious of certainty. I used to write sesquipedalian letters to future versions of myself.

To the forty-year-old version of me (i.e. you),

It strikes me suddenly as I sit here at the confident yet cynical age of somewhere between fourteen and fifteen that you (me) must by now be in one of the following dire predicaments:

1. You are a boring middle-class consumer tied down to an abstemious life with a twenty-year-old marriage and a boring job and three kids.

2. You are a three-times-divorced rich Xanthippe with a big art studio.

3. You are single, lonely and working in a science lab all day.

4. You are dead.

Now seeing as you (me) are my (your) responsibility, I (you) have come up with a back-up plan for your salvation. Here it is:

1. Quit your job.

2. You must write a book. I don't care what sort of book, but it must have a sense of humour.

3. Either quit your marriage, find a new romance, or move your life to a place far away from western consumerism (in the east) and become a missionary.

4. You must find the people you value in your life (or just pick randoms off the street and devote your life to them).

NB: If all else fails, eat a whole tub of ice cream, then give away everything you own and jump off the Sky Tower in the nude.

Yours agnostically,
Maddy

Trying to interpret my fourteen-year-old self's intentions is like trying to understand the Old Testament. I have a feeling I knew that signing off 'agnostically' contradicted my plans to become a missionary. I liked to be a contradiction. It meant nobody could be certain in their assessment of me, and why should I let anyone be certain about me when I wasn't certain about myself?

I imagined my future self as a conformist, living a shell of a life in some bland cubicle office like the people in *American Beauty*. I wanted to shock them. I imagined growing up to be like having my identity hijacked by different versions of myself. I would keep being updated like this until I couldn't change anymore, and then I would be stuck with the brain that I had, unmalleable. So I had to keep writing these letters as a way of interrupting this slow stiffening of my mind. My future self was like a Barbie doll in a Barbie house with all the accessories, and I was sending mail to future Barbie me, trying to convince her to wrench open the house I'd built her so that she could see my world again.

*

Every year, the church put on a Christmas play involving all the children, who would dress up as angels, shepherds and wise men. More often than not, because she was the minister's wife, my mum was responsible for organising and directing this event. It was one of those church events traditionally thrust upon someone who had no time for it, and because of this there was a method to pulling them off. The popular thing to do was to tell the Christmas story using a funny adaptation in a children's book. The story was told from the point of view of the barn cat who is thrown out of the manger so that baby Jesus can sleep there, or the innkeeper who keeps getting woken up by all the noisy angels and shepherds and wise men who come to visit baby Jesus in the middle of the night. The grumpy cat or innkeeper sees the holy baby and their heart melts and they are no longer annoyed about their sleep deprivation. Sleep deprivation is a relatable topic for parents in the lead-up to Christmas time. The key to the Christmas play's success is not the quality of the production, but rather the level of cuteness on the stage. A donkey mask left over from Palm Sunday could be repurposed for a two-person team to play the part of the donkey. Toddlers could be convinced to tolerate halos while roaming free along the edge of the stage. If you were lucky, the plastic-doll Jesus could be replaced with someone's newborn.

By the time we were teenagers, my sisters and I had suffered through every iteration of these children's book adaptations. We didn't go to church all the time by then, only when we were needed to play in the church band, but this included playing the Christmas carols for the Christmas play. We decided Mary deserved better. This was, after all, a teenage pregnancy drama being performed in the genre of 'musical children's bedtime story'. Every year we watched as Mary travelled a long way cross-country with someone she barely knew and then sat passively as a baby was handed to her with a cheerful round of 'Away in a Manger'. We were over it. My younger sister and I decided to co-write a new Christmas play. Our play would have dirt and blood and moody cello accompaniment. It would be a gritty realist story about a teenage girl who is forcibly impregnated by an almighty being, made to marry a family acquaintance for the sake of propriety, told 'Do not be afraid' by a glowing, supernatural angel-man, and made to travel a long distance to give birth in a dirty stable with no medical care or female relatives present. Finally she goes on the run from a tyrannical king who wants her son dead, unaware that her child is predestined to be crucified at the age of thirty-three by an angry mob, as a divinely arranged human sacrifice, while she watches helplessly. If you saw it like that, it was a story with potential. There was not much in the way of talent among the Sunday School attendees, and the stage lighting options were very basic, but we would think about that later.

Mary and Joseph had almost reached Bethlehem when we abandoned the project. Officially, we ran out of time and moved on with our obsessions. But part of it was that I was writing the play to make the story seem real to me, and we were reaching the part of the story that was most unreal: all those visitors after the birth and the shepherds seeing angels. Mostly it was the angels that bothered me. They couldn't be real multi-dimensional characters, because they were divine. They were perfect, essentially. I hated the idea of something perfect. For all the rest of it I could at least suspend my disbelief, but I didn't get angels.

'Can we make them strange birds?' I asked my sister. 'Can we imply they're just a hallucination?'

'No,' she said. 'That's stupid. It's Christmas, there are angels.'

In order to write a Christmas play, you had to tolerate angels. If you couldn't, the whole thing became intolerable, like throwing fairy godmothers into a self-help book.

Recently I was riding shotgun on a family trip. I had control of the Bluetooth speakers, so I forced my parents to listen to the entirety of Beyoncé's album *Lemonade*. I wasn't even enjoying it. I hated having control of the music since I'm as agnostic about musical genres as I am about religion and it gives me anxiety to think that others are judging my musical tastes. But since the release of *Lemonade* I'd become a #beyliever. My dad only listens to the Mountain Goats and my mum finds anything more recent than the romantic period to be 'too loud', but I wanted them to appreciate Beyoncé. I held my phone out behind me with the music video, so they could watch it from the back seats. 'Appreciate her!' I demanded. I made everyone watch it in silence as I ticked off in my head the most brilliant moments.

'Why does she say that about hot sauce in her bag?' asked Mum. 'What's hot sauce?' I gave a tentative summary of race politics in the US, which I'd learned mainly from late-night comedy shows.

'. . . and so, in a way, Beyoncé sees herself as proof that the American dream is possible for Black people too, which is why she boasts so much about her wealth,' I explained.

'Oh, I see,' said Dad, 'the American dream of economic meritocracy where virtue is equated with wealth. I knew there was something wrong I couldn't put my finger on.' I rolled my eyes. Of course, it wasn't new to me that the American dream is a delusion that demonises the poor. I'd read *The Great Gatsby*. It was just that Beyoncé's music was about more than that and I wasn't going to be able to explain it all. I decided that maybe we all choose the doctrines we can tolerate the worst parts of.

In high school, when people found out my dad was a church minister, they would ask, 'Is he very strict?' But the closest my dad came to being strict was when he frowned and said, 'Listen to your mother, girls.' Religion wasn't something one talked about in high school. If someone derisively mentioned the people intimidating young women outside abortion clinics, afterwards they'd say, 'Oh sorry, Maddy, no offence,' to which I would attempt to explain that I didn't know those people and I didn't think they had anything to do with me or my parents. The more firmly I insisted that my family weren't crazy, anti-science or secretly oppressing me, the more religious I seemed, since who would talk about religion except a religious person?

Sometimes I would ask my dad a question like 'What's Heaven supposed to look like?' and he would pause for a long time before questioning my use of the words 'supposed' and 'look', since perhaps it was not a physical space that you could look at, as such. Then I might say, 'Well, what is it then?' and he would pause for a long time before questioning the ability of anyone to imagine what lies outside our perceptual abilities. You could start with any question—how can God be love if love is not God? Why didn't God send his son to Earth during a time with the internet?—and he would take your question and complicate it and make it bigger so that it encompassed fundamental existential problems, and the whole family would be drawn in, everyone interrupting and questioning and defining, until the point where the next step in logic would require a leap of faith. And then there was no way for either side to make any further point. Luckily, by then, Mum would have reminded Dad of whatever he was supposed to have been doing in the first place, and we'd be satisfied that even though we hadn't won, none of us could yet have been said to have lost.

I noticed that other people didn't have these kinds of conversations with their parents. It wasn't the same when you tried it with friends. On my thirteenth birthday party, I put a tent up in the backyard and had two friends sleep over. I had every intention of having a normal sleepover like the girls in movies who gossip and talk about boys. Instead we debated the beginning of the universe. My point was that there were things that science couldn't explain, so you couldn't use science to prove there wasn't a god, but maybe the point got a bit garbled. My friend Rachel insisted that God was impossible and refused to accept my point. I kept saying, 'But what caused that?' and she kept trying to explain and then I would say, 'But what caused that?' and it went on until we got to the Big Bang. 'But what caused the Big Bang?' And somehow the argument kept going even after we got to the Big Bang, even though none of us, and no one else in the world, knew what had caused the Big Bang. The third friend begged us to stop, and we wanted to. We were bored and tired, but neither of us could cede our point of view.

It became morning. We were hungry. Our eyes hurt from pointing the torch at one another and our mouths hurt from talking. We hated it all but we couldn't stop.

*

'Well, abortion is killing a human being,' Dad said one afternoon, 'so shouldn't it be considered murder?'

I was twenty-three. I didn't know how the argument had started. Perhaps there had been some discussion of access to healthcare in the United States. My parents and I had been at my nana and grandad's house over the summer break and I hadn't been giving my full attention to the conversation, as I'd been researching body grease for my future as a long-distance swimmer.

'Ew,' I said. 'That's so grossly conservative of you.'

'Well, is a foetus a human being?' Dad said. 'It has all the DNA of a human being. At what point does it become human? If it's human, and you kill it, that's murder.'

'You can't just go around calling people murderers,' I said. I wasn't shouting but I wasn't using my inside voice either. Grandad and Mum carried on making dinner behind me. I could see Nana in the corner of my eye squinting at her crossword. I knew I was being disruptive, but I wanted to be hysterical. I liked to think of my dad as an oppressive patriarch from time to time, whenever it suited my desire to feel righteous.

'You can't murder someone until after they're born,' I said. 'Before that, it's foeticide. That's how murder is legally defined.'

'Well, the legal definition is not really the point, is it?'

I rolled my eyes. 'Do you agree with those pro-lifers who harass people outside of clinics?'

'They are probably not going the right way about it.' He shrugged. 'But maybe they have a point. There has to be some middle ground.'

I sighed and stormed over to the couch. 'What if the baby would have to live in poverty or grow up in an abusive household or get handed over to one of those Romanian orphanages where it would become brain-damaged from lack of attention?'

I could tell Nana agreed with me by the way she was trying to spit out her response. 'No, those orphanages are not a life, are they?' she said. She had to force each word out slowly. Motor neurone disease was destroying the muscles in her mouth. She'd only ever used her voice when she felt strongly about something in the first place, and now, whenever she wanted something known she took too long to get it out, and whoever she was talking to had already folded the washing wrong or moved into the next room to incorrectly attempt the thing they'd asked for help with, or moved swiftly forward with their argument about the value of human life.

'Is life only valuable if it's a positive experience?' said Dad.

I rolled my eyes. 'Well, what about the mother's life?'

'Of course, that matters too. She's not likely to die from the abortion, so it's a bit different.'

'This is so annoying, Dad. You're not a woman. You'll never have to make this choice.'

'Does that mean I am not allowed an opinion?'

'No, you're not,' I said.

'Every woman has a choice,' said Nana haltingly.

'Exactly,' I said. 'Mum, do you agree with this bullshit?'

'Oh well,' said Mum, 'I do think it's so easy for you young people these days to get access to abortions, and you know, the morning-after pill, etcetera.'

'What's the morning-after pill got to do with it?' I said.

'Well,' said Dad, 'since it kills the fertilised egg, it should be considered murder too, shouldn't it?'

'What?' I said. In my head I thought, What?

'Why are you taking this so personally?' he said.

'What do you mean why am I taking it fucking personally?'

38

I thought of the long walk on a Sunday morning to the urgent doctors because the pharmacies were closed. I thought of stepping into the little side room, which was not really a room but a curtained-off cubicle, and being asked personal questions and trying to answer quietly so that all the people in the very quiet waiting room on the other side of the curtain wouldn't hear. I thought of being led to the counter and handing over the $37.50 and carrying the taped-up bag with the box in it, which didn't fit in my pocket, and walking all the way home and locking myself in my room and ripping open the bag and then the box which was too large to contain a single pill. It was like when my sisters and I, as children, would wrap presents multiple times to make something tiny look large and exciting.

'I just am,' I said.

'I think we should continue this another time,' said Dad. 'I think it makes Nana and Grandad upset.' Nana and Grandad had left. Maybe they were taking it personally too.

'You're the one calling people murderers,' I said. I stomped down to the backyard. I was staying in the Hut, a back-country-style hut made out of a shipping container that Grandad had set up as an office space. I sat down in the office chair behind the big wooden desk and spun around in the chair, shaking off thoughts as if trying to unsettle flies.

'There is only one truth. That's the nature of truth,' Dad had said once. Maybe it was.

The Hut was full of mountaineering books and mountaineering photographs, and textbooks about tropical illnesses and how to perform surgery without running water or electricity. Years ago, Grandad was a missionary doctor

39

in Papua New Guinea. When he and Nana told his parents that they were going to Papua New Guinea to be Christian missionaries, his dad had got upset and said, 'What a waste of time and resources to spread such a nonsensical story.' It was only after they'd been to Papua New Guinea and seen more of the world, Grandad said, that they'd begun to see 'the nonsense side of it'. They are both Christian still, but in a corner of the Hut I noticed he had a gilded copy of the Qur'an and a book of Buddhist teachings. In the hut too are notebooks full of my grandad's poems. He writes them peppered with ellipses, as if each sentence is a glimpse of some greater submerged text. 'We believe / I believe / we both believe / creeds are worn / lost and / harsh / formulae that / exclude / by virtue of / their sense of knowing /. . . all.'

Nana and Grandad are my mum's parents. When my mum went to university, she thought her parents weren't going far enough with their faith, so she briefly became an evangelical. She went to a church where everyone jumped up and down and waved their arms in the air for the Holy Spirit and had their demons exorcised.

My dad's parents are Zionist Brethren. Their church doesn't allow women to preach. They talk lovingly of Israeli military technology, and their hall mirror proclaims in gold lettering, 'Choose THIS DAY whom you will serve. BUT as for me and my family, we will serve THE LORD.' When my dad announced, after getting his PhD in theology, that he had become a Presbyterian, his parents were scandalised. He was intensely shy and terrified of public speaking, but he insisted on becoming a church minister.

I swung on the office chair in the Hut and thought of

how philosophical rebellion ran in my family. Perhaps I was doomed to continue it. Did anyone really choose a philosophy for themselves, or was it always just one long argument with your parents?

Grandad knocked on the door of the Hut, interrupting my thoughts. He was carrying a little vase made from an old deodorant bottle, filled with wildflowers. 'This is from Nana and me,' he said. 'Nana said to tell you she thinks you're completely right. She said, "He doesn't get to have a say, because he's not a woman."' He winked, another kind of ellipsis, plonked the vase on the desk and ambled back up to the house.

I used to think agnosticism was a transitional phase. I thought it was a problem that would resolve itself one day, the way we expect to stumble across true love.

A few weeks before, I'd had one of those debates with my dad, and I said, 'Can't I just choose to make moral choices without religion?' and he said something like, 'But where does your sense of right or wrong come from, and if it is just biology behind everything, then there's no explanation for your moral behaviour except that it makes you feel better, or it betters your chance of surviving as an individual or a species.'

'No,' I said, without knowing why I was rejecting this. 'It's not just that. People can just choose to care about other people.'

'So, you agree that there is some greater reason beyond a biological imperative?'

All I knew was that I knew nothing. My dad might have said that this was oxymoronic, since knowing that you don't know is a kind of knowing. Perhaps I didn't know for sure that I didn't know anything. In other words, I might know something. In fact, I was certain I did know some things, only that these things didn't add up to a knowledge of the whole nature of anything.

But maintaining that I didn't know whether or not I knew would be nonsensical, since how could I not know the contents of my own knowledge—unless knowledge had slipped inside me undetected, for me to find when I looked hard enough, like repressed trauma or a set of keys that has been lost down the sides of a couch that hasn't been cleaned for fear of what might be found or not found. Maybe saying 'I know I don't know' was just the same as saying 'I don't know'. Maybe such a statement was unsuitably certain in its declaration.

As I swung around and around in the chair, I thought about how maybe I didn't know anymore what it meant to keep learning and also remain fundamentally ignorant. I couldn't remember what I'd learned in Classics about Socrates, whether he really believed he didn't know anything, or whether he was posing as ignorant to lure people into feeling comfortable enough to share their arguments with him, so that in his questioning he could prove that they didn't know, even when he himself couldn't make any claims to the contrary. It's easier to point out flaws in other people's arguments than to build your own hypothesis, but it also might be misguided to build a hypothesis for the sake of having a hypothesis. Such hypotheses are, like Netflix binges, a comfortable rest for the brain. In this way my ignorance was not passive. I stayed in the dark for a while, in the office chair, lifting my feet so that the chair kept moving.

Rules

The Computer Game

You are the computer. Your sister is the only one who can operate the computer. First, she has to say 'Power on' and press you on the nose. You have to say 'Please enter password'. And she has to guess, and she has to be wrong and you have to offer her a hint, and the hint should be something that only she will be able to guess, and when she has guessed it, you have to say 'Loading desktop' and your hands should do a little robotic dance to indicate the loading process, and then you have to say 'Welcome to the computer. Please select a task from the menu'. And she'll always select 'Games', which she knows how to do by pressing a knee or an elbow and saying 'Games', and then you have to say 'Games menu. Please select a game'. And then she should press somewhere, like a shoulder blade or a belly button or a pinkie finger, and you will say 'You have selected'—and you can say anything you like then, and she has to play the game. You could say 'Interpretive dance-off' and she'd have to dance to your mother's baroque mix-tapes, illustrating concepts with increasing levels of difficulty, beginning with 'anger', then 'popcorn', 'electricity', and finally 'love'. Or you could say 'The floor is lava. You have survived a volcanic eruption and must save your family's valuables without falling to your death'. And she will have to rescue items in increasing levels of danger from the surrounding lava, beginning with the salt and pepper shakers, and ending with the dog, who, unaware of the danger, will have to be saved before he leaps off the couch to his death. Or you can say 'Time travel' and she will be transported thousands of years into the past where she has to escape a Tyrannosaurus Rex, and you have to robotically reassemble yourself into the T-Rex, and she'll run.

Then she has to win the game, and return to the Games menu, and then you have to say 'Games menu. Please select a game'.

The Sleeping Bag Game

The sleeping bag goes over your head and covers your entire body. Your sisters spin you around and around until you have lost all sense of where you are. You must now reach your father's library at the far end of the house, trapped in this feet-smelling polyester cocoon. All noises are suffocated out, only your own battle cry to carry you on. But your body tries to carry you in a circle instead of the way you direct it. You spin around again, the way they spun you, their phantom hands pushing you on further detours while they stand laughing.

The Mediation Game

You have to catch the moment the argument was conceived, which is always several minutes or even hours before either of your parents are aware they are having an argument.

It might be, for instance, that your dad has forgotten something, forgotten that your mum needed the car that day, forgotten to take in the laundry, forgotten that he needed to drop one of you off at orchestra practice, and she has had to remind him at the last minute even though she is tired because she has had a long day, and he has said, 'Oh, that's right, orchestra practice,' and she has given a twitch of both eyebrows. It is the twitch that you have to look for, as if she is trying to shake something off her prefrontal cortex.

Some time later, he will ask her an unrelated administerial question which belongs, in her mind, to the category of things he should know by now. And she will make a generalisation about his incompetence, for which he will request further data as support for her claim. In response, she will refer to his almost forgetting the orchestra practice drop-off earlier, to which she will add, 'And I cleaned the whole house after I came back from work, and I made dinner, and my wrist hurts,' and at this point it will begin to be difficult to follow the argument, as it builds up steam and moves swiftly away from the subject about which it began, but you have to stay on your game. If you stay on your game, you will notice when your mum will say something like, 'I just wish you'd X.'

And Dad will say something like, 'Well, that's ridiculous, how does X relate to the administerial question about which this argument started?'

At this point you can jump in and answer your dad's question by saying to him, 'Don't you see that Mum is not literally arguing about the subject that she's arguing about, and that she cannot understand the logical argument you have attempted to present because she has her ear tuned to the frequency of feelings, and therefore any logical counter-argument is unproductive and merely serves as a performance of righteousness which makes her feel that you are not listening to her feelings?' And you can say to your mum, 'Don't you see that you are speaking in response to a subterranean hurt which has existed within you for most of our childhoods like a disused subway system, built decades ago and never properly dismantled, even long after the trains have stopped running?' and once you have said these things you can stop listening because you have won your parents' argument.

Speculative Fiction

There was a bird in Cape Town that sang often. In the evenings as I lay in bed I could hear it, and in the mornings, just outside the window of the office where I worked as an intern. 'Hooo hooo ha ha hooo,' it said.

'What's that bird?' I asked Alexine, the intern I was interning for.

'What bird?'

'You'll hear it again. Wait.' Sure enough, it came again, an identical sequence like Morse code. 'Hooo hooo ha ha hooo.'

'That one.'

'Oh, I don't know, I've never noticed it.'

I didn't understand how she could not have noticed it. But then, perhaps it's a cultural thing, what you pay attention to. Alexine was from Belgium, which was pretty much wall-to-wall cities. One time I asked her how Belgium was formed, and she wasn't sure. 'Is it normal to know that sort of thing?' she asked. And yet she was much smarter than me and almost had her master's in clinical psychology.

That afternoon when I went home to the flat I was living in, I asked our cleaner, who was South African, what the bird was. I tried reproducing its sound for her. She thought I was very funny.

'Eh, I never hear a bird,' she said, chuckling. 'You tell those girls to do their dishes.'

The bird haunted me all day and night for the two months I was in South Africa, and I could never see it no matter how carefully I searched the trees outside the windows.

When I was a child, I looked for signs of magic everywhere— hidden doors, strange beetles, circular arrangements of fungi. I'd pick up bits of paper off the side of the road in case they held secret messages. When we were tramping I'd stay behind for a moment on a quiet patch of the track and stand very still, waiting for whatever lived there to stop hiding and return to its usual affairs. I'd say, 'Hello, I know you're watching me' when nobody was around, to catch off-guard any invisible creatures that might be following me.

In South Africa, magic was everywhere. The first night I arrived, a homeless man lifted a metal hatch in the footpath and showed me his secret stash of biblical pamphlets. He said there was a network of homeless people who kept things in the footpaths. Driving along the highway I glimpsed a group of cloaked men approaching each other at sunset in an empty field and took them for wizards preparing for a duel. And once, everybody on my train leaped from their seats in fear simultaneously, and none of us were able to name the source of our panic.

The moment my plane landed in South Africa, my nose began to bleed. Blood gushed into my hands as I waited for the seatbelt sign to turn off. As I walked across the runway, the blood dried on my face and hands. Driving from the airport to the flat I would share with other foreign interns, I saw a township for the first time. It was a dense area of corrugated sheds pressed against the roadside with a spider's web of wires overhead. Andrew, the cheerful local man in charge of my internship placement, was driving me and he said a township was like what in other countries was called a slum. These townships had been created to segregate people during apartheid, but they remained because their residents still had no way out of poverty. I had never considered the idea that economic apartheid did not stop when legal apartheid did.

As soon as I arrived in my new neighbourhood, I went to the grocery store and discovered that my money could buy ten times as much as it could in New Zealand. Effectively, I was now rich. I did not know how to handle either the giddy freedom of being able to do or buy anything I wanted or the power it brought me. I became a target.

It began the moment I stepped out of my new flat to walk to the store and didn't stop till the day I flew home. Beggars followed me down the street, pleading. There was a woman with a tumour the size of an eggplant on her throat. She said she didn't want to die of starvation before she died of cancer, and, knowing the beliefs that tourists were likely to hold about beggars, offered to buy the food with my money as I watched, to prove that was what she was using it for. There was a woman

49

who ran up to me crying on the street where I lived. She was crying so hard she found it difficult to speak, and I had trouble making sense of her words. She sat down in the gutter, put her baby on the sidewalk and started changing his nappy as she tried to explain that her husband had brought her here from Zimbabwe and then abandoned her with two small children and no way to pay her rent. I sat beside her and tried to listen, but I didn't know what to say. I went into my house and came back with enough money for her week's rent and the phone number for a helpline I had found by googling. But as I walked away I knew I had failed her. She didn't thank me, and I didn't want her to. I was supposed to be a psychology intern. I'd studied psychology for three years but was incapable of saying anything useful when it mattered. When I returned to my flat, upset, I told my flatmates what had happened.

'You shouldn't have given her anything,' they said. 'If you keep helping them, they'll keep coming back here. You don't owe them anything. You can't help everyone.' This was common advice passed around by tourists here, and even though I couldn't agree with the philosophy, over time the sheer number of these encounters began to defeat me. The more that beggars followed me down the street the easier it became to ignore them, to stop thinking about them. It became easier to focus on other things. After all, there were many other voices on the streets too—taxi drivers and people selling fruit or crafts, or just shouting for reasons I couldn't determine, as if it were Armistice Day and they were the first to know. The city had an overwhelming feeling of freedom and possibility, a sort of magic that I'd sensed from the first day, and I couldn't detect its source. Maybe it was to do with scale. I had never been in a city this large. We had rooftop pool parties and climbed mountains where we could see the whole city all the way to the sea. We walked through markets where the crowds were overwhelming. Once, we went to a Secret Sunset, an event sponsored by a brand of coconut water, where we roared like lions in the sunset and danced with our eyes closed, each of us with headphones on so that to anyone passing by we looked like strangers screaming, but everyone who could hear the music and the instructor was transformed into something bigger. I wanted to write all of it down and keep it, everything I saw in Cape Town; they were all what were called 'experiences' and therefore they felt valuable in some way. Horror and wonder, when experienced from a position of safety, become difficult to differentiate.

My internship was a dead end, but I always felt that the next day would be the day something happened. Two weeks in, I'd been reassigned to a different workplace— the South African National Council for Alcohol and Drug Rehabilitation (SANCA). My new supervisor, the clinical psychologist I'd been hoping to shadow, resigned soon after I started working there, which was why I was left interning for her intern, Alexine. Alexine was further on in her education than me, so she was qualified to meet with clients. I was not, but with the clients' consent I was allowed to sit in on some of her meetings. Alexine herself did not have much work to begin with, because her clients often failed to show up for their appointments. Most of her clients were addicts, and when they did attend it was often grudgingly, for example because their school principal had sent them to SANCA under threat of expulsion. This did not make for a high attendance rate.

We planned our trips to the shops across the road. We discussed Alexine's diet, which consisted of meal replacement shakes and lemon water. She was a stronger person than I would ever be, because on top of this inhuman diet she had a second internship in the evenings and weekends. Yet she was still fun to be around. There are certain people who have a way about them that invites unfiltered self-expression simply because they don't shut it down. Perhaps it's the therapist's knack. We compared Belgium and New Zealand. I explained about Belgian biscuits. She'd never heard of them. Once, after two no-show appointments, I suggested that I should just pretend to be a client, and she could pretend to rehabilitate me. Then I performed my own style of modern dance for her. She would have to think of a noun, and I would attempt to embody the spirit of that noun.

'Table,' she said obligingly, and I started making heavy wooden movements, my back parallel to the floor, my arms and legs lumbering, shaking, stepping back and forth in a dopey Irish jig fashion.

'Bubble,' she said and I leapt out of table stance and pirouetted with my arms in fifth position.

We visited the dog who was perpetually chained up by the gate. He was old and smelly, but he nuzzled my lap as I scratched behind his ear, in that hungry way of old dogs who lack attention. One day the dog wasn't there, and we asked the guard where he had gone. The guard said he'd gone to live 'on the other side', only he pointed over the fence as he was saying it. I began to wonder if there was a house on the other side of the fence with a big yard where the dog was living out his last years.

I decided to write a novel. I'd never written anything longer than a short story before. I knew about the sunk cost fallacy, but I wanted the money I had already spent getting to South Africa to feel like it had achieved something. My novel would be about South Africa, in particular about a woman who worked at a drug rehabilitation centre in Cape Town.

I began by writing the world around me, so, by necessity, I began with conjecture. I imagined what had happened to the dog. I wondered whether the bird I heard was an omen. I tried to imagine the children who used to live in the children's home before it was converted into this office space. I wondered about the cleaner, whose name was Princess. She was a tall woman with three long scars on her cheek that looked like the gouge marks of Wolverine's claws. Princess's job was to clean this small group of offices, and she seemed to be employed almost full-time. With some difficulty in communication, I had helped her create a Facebook account. When I returned her greeting with 'Ndiphilile, enkosi, unjani?' ('I'm fine thanks, how are you?'), she was so thrilled that I was taken aback. 'These other girls not even try to learn,' she said. Princess had a sense of pride in her work. She moved at a leisurely pace from room to room. She always had a duster or a vacuum cleaner in hand, leaving the spaces just dusty enough to provide work for herself in the future. Once a day, she would kick the social workers and therapists out of their offices one by one, when they had no clients, so she could clean their offices.

I wondered about the clients. Even though, in a way, it was my job to wonder about them, mostly there was so little information to latch on to that I couldn't hope to adequately imagine their lives. Like any budding psychologist I wanted a puzzle with all of the pieces already present. Sitting in on other people's therapy sessions is like participating in a low-budget crime show that you know will be cancelled before the end of its first season, except the client is both the culprit and the victim, and rather than pitting criminal masterminds against brilliant detectives, both client and therapist feel inadequate in their roles. Alexine's clients didn't give much away, answering 'Yes' or 'No', participating just enough to be considered participating. A typical case might be a boy of fourteen who'd been caught smoking weed. Even though it's not chemically addictive, we were required to treat dagga (weed) with the same intervention techniques as if it were alcohol or Mandrax or tic (meth). This boy might have been smoking dagga since he was eleven, and heavily since thirteen. He didn't get upset or express any strong emotion. He didn't mind being there, answering 'Yes' or 'No', writing the little exercises that Alexine gave him, but he didn't want to quit smoking. He smoked because he was bored, he said, and he didn't like his friends. He had dropped out of his sports team and said it was because his shoes broke, but Alexine suspected that smoking had affected his breathing. We'd never find out, as he didn't return after his third session.

At first, I thought my main character should be a white tourist, a foreigner. It was the only real perspective available to me. I didn't know how to think like a South African. It would be a convenient way to work with all the South African material I had been gathering. This character could visit South Africa, get caught up in a plot that would entangle them somehow in a strange new community, a web of magic and threat. Mysteries would unravel with answers revealing themselves at the end. Then, I supposed the only thing to do to my protagonist short of having them get lost in South Africa and never find their way home would be to have them learn something and then go home a different person. I had hopes that by the time I was flying home to New Zealand I would know what the protagonist had learned. It would be like planning an Easter egg hunt in a stranger's garden, discovering each secret of the landscape just in time for your egg-hunter to discover it after you.

My sandals were breaking apart. I had worn the same shitty pair for a month and a half, and I had taken to not wearing them at all. I was growing hard callouses on my feet. They could withstand the temperatures of almost melting tarseal. I had read that you absorb nutrients from the soil by walking barefoot, and I was convinced that eventually my feet would become as durable and as sensitive to information retrieved through the soil as the paws of great cats. When Alexine and I decided to walk to the mall on our lunch break, I left my sandals in my bag and pranced off down the gravel driveway to the road.

'You're crazy,' said Alexine.

'Yes,' I said, 'but I'm free.'

South African tarseal is not the most nutritious of substances, even if my theory were true, but there was a certain toxicological appeal to feeling every hardened smear and strange shiny residue press against my toes.

When we returned, Princess and the receptionist, Nombequ, saw me in my bare feet. They started laughing.

'I think this is a white people thing,' said Nombequ. 'Black people always wear shoes.'

'Why is that?' I asked.

She took a minute to answer. 'A white girl walking without shoes is one thing, people will just think you are crazy. If a black girl were to walk around without shoes like that though, those same people will assume she is too poor for shoes.'

I decided to take myself out of my novel. Maybe scrubbing off any sign of my own perspective would allow South Africa to take my place as a character and speak for itself. I knew that my perspective wasn't enough to see what was really going on, but maybe the problem would be solvable, if only I could zoom out enough from where I was standing.

One day I noticed a boy in the waiting room. He was five or six years old, and he was eating a bag of orange cheesy chips that looked like Cheezels. There was a smattering of fine orange powder on the carpet around him. His mother sat behind him, picking her nail polish off chip by chip, waiting. I stored up Cheezel Boy in my head, and for some reason, he stuck. In my novel, Cheezel Boy's mum, Mbali, is addicted to Mandrax and comes to the clinic regularly for drug rehabilitation counselling. I invented a counsellor named Camille, who is very stressed because her sister, a recovering addict, has asked her for money and won't explain why. Camille is increasingly unable to relate to her clients. Sometimes, when she looks at them, she can only see her sister. She feels a secret, uncontrollable rage towards her clients; she can't help thinking they are simply weak, despite what she knows about the processes of addiction.

Mbali says she doesn't want to stay in the new state house that Camille has spent weeks fighting for her to be given. It is safely distant from the drug ring that Mbali has been involved in, and her best chance to stay sober.

'I don't like it there,' she tells Camille. 'It's too quiet.'

At this moment, Camille, who is sleep-deprived, has an almost hallucinatory moment, believing she is speaking to her sister, and she says something very unprofessional. Mbali is upset and leaves with her son.

The next day, Cheezel Boy wakes up and his mother is missing. Feeling guilty, Camille spends the weekend trying to help the boy track down Mbali.

The problem began when the world of the story had to expand beyond these precipitating events. I could imagine what might occur in some version of the counselling clinic where I worked. But my characters all came from the townships. I had only been in a township once, during my previous internship posting in a guarded hospital facility. I had left the compound only once, and only for a few minutes when I had forgotten my lunch. Most of what I knew about the townships was gleaned from driving past Khayelitsha on the highway.

I didn't know what the inside of a shack looked like, how people who lived there talked to one another, how people found their way around without roads or how people showered. I didn't know how people travelled to their jobs, what happened when you went to see a sangoma or traditional healer, how religions were actually practised, what schools looked like or what slang sounded like. I knew from driving past that in many cases toileting facilities were a line of communal portaloos along the fence, but that most of the shacks were set up with satellite TV. I knew that small herds of goats were guarded by children on the strips of grass beside the motorways. I knew that a sangoma could cure impotence and I knew the phone number for a hairdryer repairman. Beyond these facts, the world my characters stumbled through was a hazy void into which pieces of New Zealand took up residence. When I wrote Camille's childhood, I saw her hiding on the roof of the bike shed at my first primary school and sneaking through the gap in the hedge that I remembered bordering my own school. In my childhood, on the other side of the hedge were the grounds of the Anzac Memorial garden and the church where my dad had preached. In my novel, the other side of the hedge was a piece of rubbish-strewn wilderness, like something I had seen on the side of a motorway. I was constructing my fictional South Africa from the corners of highways sewn together with my own memories. Camille, as a teenager, had a friend who invited her to his house and showed her his father's gun, and, in a box under the couch cushions, something secret and very old that had been inherited. I didn't know what this would be when I began writing the scene, but when Camille reached in her hand to feel what was in the box, she felt feathers. She lifted out something stiff and feathery, and in my head it was a cloak, a green and brown feathery cloak, like that which might belong to a powerful Māori chief.

I decided to set the book in the future instead, in a fictional future Cape Town. I was retreating into the future, where the facts were sure to loosen their grip.

Cape Town is an island. Table Mountain takes centre stage in the island, and the water is encroaching, each new tide washing out more of the townships. The rich have taken ownership of the mountain and built houses on it to protect themselves from the floods, which shrink the island slowly, creating new waves of homelessness and overcrowding. When Camille is a child, she lives in an outer township area. Her father tells her the myth of Table Mountain—that it is a giant who was sent to guard the southern corner of the world. The giant died and turned to rock, and now is watching over them all, making sure the sea monsters stay away.

I returned home to New Zealand. The plane trip took two days, including twelve hours in the Dubai airport in the early hours of the morning in which I became so muddled in my decision-making that I paid sixty dollars for a thirty-minute massage from a mechanical chair. By the time I was back in the Dunedin airport I barely remembered who I was. I had been in an airport for my entire life. It was raining in Dunedin and I couldn't handle the change of temperature. The whole world was shrinking and becoming stiff with frost, and I was stranded, two days and thousands of dollars away from anywhere worth being.

A few days later I heard that Andrew, the man who had organised my internship, a friendly bear-hugging South African guy I had hiked with in the Cederberg Mountains, had been hit by a car while walking along the sidewalk, and died. I began to realise that my experience in Cape Town, which had been soaked in a sense of opportunity and magic, the feeling that anything could happen, was an experience I had bought. It wouldn't have existed without the company that had organised activities for me and the people I had lived and explored with who had come from their own countries with the same ache for adventure. It dawned on me that magic is just anything that doesn't have a logical cause or explanation.

Cape Town is magic to foreigners because we can't see the explanations. This isn't really magic; it's a sort of blindness.

I felt it all evaporate. I was unemployed. I didn't have anything to show from my internship and I had nothing in my future apart from what I could create with my own mind. I threw all my energy into the novel.

In the story of Camille's childhood, her dad loses his job, becomes depressed and stops speaking. The sea advances further and the township where Camille lives is forced to evacuate, but her mother refuses to move. Instead they build a second storey on their container house and live up there, as if on a houseboat, climbing down and wading through the floodwaters in gumboots every morning to go to school. Now, the island nation was run by gangs with complicated methods of extorting people to turn against their friends and families, and chains of assassins who report to other assassins, with no one knowing who they were taking orders from. The world I was creating became grimmer with every page. It wasn't the world of possibility in the face of hardship that I had encountered in South Africa, but something more cynical.

Sitting in the university library without access to the internet, since I was no longer a student there, I pushed my characters onwards in their journey through their dystopian city. Camille, having developed a sharp pain in her gut from something she later discovers is a tumour, and having not slept in a week, falls off a train, leaving Cheezel Boy to fend for himself. Camille's sister is found to be a member of the gang who kidnapped Mbali. Drones whizz overhead.

I tried to plan the methods of a notorious gang of assassins. Waking up in the middle of the night, I had an epiphany.

These gang members would work by using drones to find information on others, which they'd use to threaten them. They would send an anonymous email telling the recipient that they had to recruit new members by using their own surveillance on their friends and neighbours. It was a pyramid scheme of gang membership that had infiltrated every community on the island. No one could trust anyone. Meanwhile, Camille's coworker would discover that Camille hadn't handed over the boy to the government for placement in the foster system and was about to inform the gang. My protagonists were in a dire situation and I didn't know how to save them.

I had interview after interview for customer service jobs I was unqualified for. I began avoiding human contact. There were days where I didn't leave my flat and only left my bedroom in the dead of night to sneak downstairs to the fridge. As a last resort I would put on a coat with a hood and walk to McDonald's or to the 24-hour dairy, careful not to look at anyone, believing that they believed me to be everything I suspected myself of being. I dreaded standing there alone at McDonald's at 2am, when only groups of drunk students were about, and all the time I imagined they pitied or were disgusted by me. As soon as I got my food I would walk fast back along the road, head down, hiding the food under my arm and taking it quietly into my flat and upstairs to my room, where I would eat it secretly in my bed, which I had built on stilts as a mezzanine floor above the sea of mess below. My room was about the size of a walk-in wardrobe.

*

When I was fourteen I wagged school with my friend, an exchange student named Sara who lived with my family. We went back home and snuck in while my dad worked at the computer in our hallway, oblivious. We snuck past into our room, and I set myself up in my wardrobe with *Harry Potter and the Order of the Phoenix*, a Marmite jar of water, an axe in case of an emergency, a torch and a pillow. This wardrobe was a creaky plywood cupboard with four wooden feet and a bolt on the door and just enough room to sit down in. The door could only close when it was bolted and the bolt could only be shut from the outside. Sara locked me in, went back to school for the next four or five hours, then came home and unlocked me at the end of the school day. The idea was that I would be completely hidden if my dad should for whatever reason want to look in my room. So, for the rest of the day, I read *Harry Potter* and was perfectly happy. Magic is the experience of being in suspense, in suspense of disbelief, in suspense of knowledge or explanation. You might really be in a cupboard, but inside that suspense anything could happen. A letter could be addressed to your very cupboard and delivered by a mysterious bird, summoning you to a world where love might conquer death.

Disappearing from real life to read about people watching their friends being murdered by cloaked wizard-Nazis is called escapism. Cloaked teleporting murderers are easier to deal with than real life, in the same way that travelling to a foreign country is easier than figuring out what to do next in one's home country. There is an incredible sense of safety in someone else's country. It's as if nothing can really get you when you have a home to go back to. But my novel wasn't someone else's country. It was no longer an escape for me.

I continued to throw conflict upon conflict at my protagonist. Maybe one day, if I wrote enough chapters, my
protagonist would start making her own decisions, or the
magic of Cape Town would kick in with a solution. I had heard
of it happening—characters coming to life like imaginary
friends for their authors. But Camille was too tired to help
me out. She was wandering robotically through the streets
of a futuristic island of fear and isolation with a pain in her
chest and an exhaustion that made her barely capable of basic
functions. She wasn't a person. She was a set of characteristics,
life events and places. Was the problem that I had made her
too different from myself? But the problem was larger than
that. I had tried to return to the magic I'd felt in Cape Town by
creating a system of explanations. In doing so I had destroyed
the magic and replaced it, not with knowledge, which I did not
have, but with myself. I wasn't Camille. I was the island which
wasn't Cape Town. I was the dead giant of Table Mountain,
looking out at the sea of monsters, watching it encroach.
Trapped in my dwindling ecosystem, my characters didn't
have a chance.

The Scare-Cat

Our mum was famous for her strawberries, or that's what she said, and sometimes the people from church showed us the picture in the paper of us with the famous strawberries, which they had cut out to put on their refrigerators. Our mum's strawberries were big as door knobs; they had extra limbs; sometimes they had conjoined twins. Once there was one that looked exactly like the donkey-made-of-two-people that Jesus rode on Palm Sunday.

I remember the man from the paper coming to take the picture.

'You got three little strawberry blondes in your strawberry patch!' He grinned as he adjusted his camera. A single line of sweat was sliding off his spotted bald egg of a head. 'How did they crop up?'

My sisters and I didn't laugh, and carried on weeding. We

were not blondes, we were gingers. The man took a couple of photos to fill the silence.

'Your strawberry blondes,' said the man from the paper again, and I had been going to help Mum out until she followed it up with her own joke. 'Oh yes, well, they eat a strawberry for every weed they pick.' Which is not even true, my sisters and I thought telepathically to each other. We made sure we were picking two weeds for every strawberry.

In the picture that appeared in the newspaper, all eyes are on the strawberries, except for the eyes of the scare-cat. The scare-cat looks right out of the picture. She looks at everyone. She is black and thin as paper and her eyes twist green and red. The scare-cat could look out of both sides of her head. My sister said the scare-cat was just a cut-out metal thing and her eyes were just marbles. But the scare-cat had powers. Birds, cats and rats looked her in the eye and were so electrified with fear they ran away and never came back. When nobody was looking, the scare-cat leaped and tip-toed, twitched her tail and repositioned herself. She had a lot of garden to patrol. Once, out of the corner of my eye I saw her look at me and I felt the shock of it, the electric punch of her eyes—even though it didn't work on humans, or that's what Mum had said.

Mum had powers of her own. Her eyes were the same pale blue as Lake Pukaki, where our uncle drowned himself when I was too little to remember. Sometimes she would startle and take a terrified breath as if the world was about to run out of air, and say, 'Don't do that,' and pull me or my sisters away from the thing we were doing. We would be caught suddenly in her eyes and the pupils would disappear in the lake, and we would get a shock of fear—it would *zoop* right into us, from her eyes to our own.

The scare-cat kept away the strays. We had to keep away the stray cats, Mum said, because they'd get out of control and invite their friends and throw a party in the chicken coop.

Once, I went to get the eggs and found a chicken deflated on the ground with its wing snapped back the wrong way. Later it was buried in the garden near the compost heap, which was a waste, Dad said, because we could have had roast chicken for dinner. Now all I could think was that there was a dead roast chicken under there in the dirt, going bad. All because of the stray cats, which were out of control having out-of-control parties, mating and fighting and doing the same things as the motorcycle gang from next door.

We set traps for the strays in the backyard, cat-sized boxes, rough wood and a little grate, and meat at the end, and mostly the cats were too smart. But there was a day when I was running super-fast through the garden, fast as though I were lifting off, the soles of my feet digging into the bark, and I almost fell on the box and it hissed. It hissed so loud I was flung back to my feet again mid-fall, the electricity of the hiss like a forcefield. The box shook and howled. I glanced just long enough to see in the little grate—an eye! I ran.

When I came back with Mum and my sisters trailing, I saw that it wasn't as big as I'd thought. It was small and scraggly. It was a kitten!

'Mum, it's a kitten and it's scared!' we said. 'Can we let it go and find its mummy?' We knew what our mother was capable of. We had seen her crushing the snails in a bucket with a brick, picking them off the sides of the bucket when they climbed out and throwing them back. You had to be tough to grow the best strawberries.

Eventually she let us put the kitten in the conservatory to see if it would calm down, so we left the box in the middle of the glass room with the clothes rack. Mum opened the door to the box quietly and stepped back into the lounge, shutting the glass door behind her. From the lounge, we watched. At first, the kitten didn't notice she was free. Then she started backing out of the box, her little black body shrinking and extending like a Slinky, hissing, balled up. Her head came out last, and she let out a scream. She ran into the laundry basket, bowling it sideways into a chair, hurled herself out of the basket, threw herself against the glass and bounced back, then hunched in the middle of the room, her hair three times her size, like a porcupine. When I looked in her eyes, I bristled all the way through too. The kitten took up the whole room. I understood then how the scare-cat who patrolled our garden got her power. Fear is conducted through the eyes.

'I'm sorry, girls,' our mum said. 'She's already learnt how to be wild. If we let her go she'll grow up and have a lot of kittens and spread diseases and kill all the birds. She'll be a nuisance. We have to call the animal control man.'

Everything I remember after that about the kitten is not true. It is not true because I have asked my mother, and she said, 'Of course not, they would never do that!' and when I looked in her eyes, I could see exactly how wrong the memory was, which moments before had seemed normal.

But still, I remember it. A sack was hanging from the washing line with the kitten in it and I could hear it yowling and we were both afraid, because we were connected now, the kitten and me. I remember a man arriving in a big white van. He had a rifle and he pointed it at the yowling, writhing sack and shot it twice and the sack went still and limp. Blood seeped out of the sack and dripped onto the concrete path. The man picked up the sack off the line as if he were folding his washing and put it in the van. He uncocked his rifle. He put his rifle onto the seat beside him in his van and he drove away.

Khayelitsha Takeaway

'Are you lost, white girl?' someone called out to me. I smiled and shook my head in the direction of the voice, but I probably just looked confused.

I was lost. Even though it was my fifth day as an intern at this hospital, I wouldn't have been surprised if I'd walked the halls in a full circle and was about to enter the reception room I'd begun in. The white corridor seemed to be repeating itself. There were few signs, and none in English. There were no windows, and everywhere people were gently repositioning their bodies against the walls and into the chairs that lined the corridor. At intervals the corridor would expand into larger halls with rows of what looked like repurposed church pews, where more people waited. Because I never arrived before 10am, it seemed as if these people had always been there. They'd been waiting since the gates opened that morning and many would wait all afternoon. Now and again, a nurse would pop their head around the door of one of the little rooms and call out a name, and someone would stand up and follow them in.

Some looked up to watch me pass. From the expectant way they were looking, it occurred to me that they might have mistaken me for a doctor. *They might think I am a doctor because I am white.* It was a strange thought to have for the first time, as if I'd never been white before. But I'd never been the only white person. Though the doctors in Khayelitsha township were certainly not all white, there were few white people here who weren't doctors or professionals, and none who lived here.

Others fixed their eyes to the wall. They seemed relaxed, perhaps because they had come here expecting to wait. Flies drifted lazily on the weak draught and resettled on an arm or a forehead and were not batted away. I had been in Cape Town for little more than a week, and already I had noticed the difference in the way people queued. In New Zealand, if things were going slowly, people would begin to mutter and huff. Here, I had been in a queue for two hours at an electronics shop while the unhurried shop assistant chatted to another customer, and the queue ahead of me waited silently, without any indication of frustration.

Finding myself in the correct stretch of corridor at last, I opened the door to room 26 and stepped cautiously into the psychiatric office, which was the size of a small bathroom. Sister K, the psychiatric nurse, glanced at me briefly before she continued to speak in Xhosa to the patient across from her.

'Molweni,' I said. The patient looked at me and shifted uncomfortably. I shrank into the corner. Presumably, what Sister K said next was an explanation for my sudden appearance in the middle of their appointment. I heard the word 'American' and wanted to correct her. But what difference did it make? I didn't understand how she explained my presence. What would she say? 'She's here to observe without your consent but she doesn't speak Xhosa, so don't worry'? I felt like apologising, every time, but I didn't know the word for that.

Sister K wore a uniform: a heavy navy suit jacket and skirt, with a white blouse buttoned to the top. She wore the same thing every day for those few weeks I was there at the end of the South African summer. She never removed the suit jacket. I suspected that the shirt was not a whole shirt, but just a shirt-front built into the suit. This was incredible to me—I myself wore only the lightest of dress pants, a loose shirt, and jandals. That room might not have got much sunlight from the skinny frosted window, but it still felt like the inside of a just-popped bag of microwaved popcorn.

I unpacked my notepad and pencil, put my bag in the cabinet, and took up my seat at the back of the room. Maybe I could've been a convincing fake, like Leonardo DiCaprio in that movie where he pretends to be a doctor, except Sister K knew I had nothing to write. She must have known—she knew I didn't speak Xhosa. On the first day of my internship, she'd asked, 'Do you speak Xhosa?' and I said I didn't. And she said, 'Well, then, how are you going to learn?'

'I don't know,' I said. When I was offered an internship, I hadn't figured it would be my job to work that out. I had asked for a psychology internship with a clinical psychologist, paying an organisation to arrange it for me. I had hoped that it would help me figure out whether clinical psychology was the career for me. This organisation, which operated out of Cape Town and had many connections there, promised to find me a personalised internship. There were few opportunities anywhere in the world for psychology internships open to people who weren't already enrolled in a master's programme, yet how was I supposed to know whether I wanted to spend two years and thousands more dollars getting my master's if I had no idea what being a practising psychologist was really like? I'd been ecstatic when the organisation offered me a place in a 'psychology department' where I would get to 'do more than observe and ask questions', even 'make a tangible difference'. I'd been told that people would speak English around me, that the language barrier wouldn't be a problem. Instead I had been placed in this psychiatric office, unable to understand what was going on and increasingly uncomfortable as a bystander in other people's appointments. Sister K did not care one bit that I had been offered an internship here, and I had no doubt now that it hadn't been her choice. My placement organisation had paid money to the hospital, and in a hospital in which crutches were constructed out of old sticks by physicians, nobody really had a choice. On that first day, she'd looked at me like I was a toddler she had been asked to babysit.

'You can sit there,' she said. 'Put your bag in the cabinet there. We keep it hidden for safety, okay?'

So I put my bag in the cabinet, and sat in this chair, and it had been this way every day since. I'd emailed someone at my placement organisation to request a new internship. They'd emailed me back, insisting I speak to Sister K about it, and when I said I had, they promised to drop by and 'resolve the issue' with the hospital, though I could not see how it could easily be resolved. Nothing had yet happened, and in the meantime, I was told to remain.

Sister K was speaking in Xhosa, a stream of words at a low murmur. In Xhosa there are clicks which accompany certain consonants, so that it almost sounds as if the clicking comes from a different source.

The patient was a chubby woman, her skin shining with the day's sweat. She was dressed in a lavender shirt, a darker purple skirt and a headscarf to match. She spoke softly into the middle of Sister K's desk. Sister K nodded, spoke briefly, and the woman murmured, 'Enkosi, Sister,' and left the room. Sister K wrote silently for a few seconds, then got up and leaned out the door to shout for the next in line.

When I first arrived, I tried asking her questions between patients. 'Is that catatonic patient schizophrenic?' 'Where do they go with their referral?' But there's a limit to the questions you can ask when you can barely tell, in the river of exchanges, where one word ends and the next begins. She would answer my questions in as few words as possible and then go back to her work. I once asked if she could ask some of the patients to speak English, but I felt uncomfortable requesting it. 'They are not comfortable speaking English,' she said, and I knew that it was not just the difficulty of the language she meant. Often, the patients would swivel their chairs just slightly to face away from me. I was an imposition, a tourist who'd paid to view strangers at their most vulnerable without their consent in a facility that didn't have the resources to accommodate me, and everyone knew it before I did. Yet if I didn't turn up, the organisation might say that I had dropped out without trying to make it work and they might refuse to find me a more suitable internship.

Patients came in, talked for five minutes, then received their prescription or their referral to the psychiatrist, who came every Friday for a few hours. Once or twice, as I found out when the Afrikaner psychiatrist was here for those four hours each week when everybody spoke English, staff from other departments would refer patients who had chronic back pain or a bad wrist to the psychiatric department, because they didn't know how to deal with them or didn't want to.

When the psychiatrist wasn't here on those few hours on a Friday, it dragged on like this, five minutes after five minutes all day, every day, and nobody ever seemed upset about only getting five minutes, and nobody raised their voice or cried or hugged each other or slammed their fists on the table—only the gentle murmur, and Sister scribbling with her pen and nodding, and forgiving smiles on both sides. I tried to guess who had the back pain, and who had clinical depression.

An elderly woman came with four people whom I guessed to be her husband, daughter, granddaughter and grandson. All the chairs were dragged out for them from the corners, and one from the next room. The daughter spoke. She had a hand on the old woman's back, and the woman smiled and looked blankly as if her eyes were inked onto old paper.

Sister K turned to the old woman.

'Molo, Bathandwa,' she said. She said something else, and Bathandwa smiled but did not speak when Sister K paused.

The daughter said something. I heard the word 'English' and shook myself awake.

'You want to speak English?' Sister K asked Bathandwa,

74

and I wasn't sure if she had asked on my behalf, or if the girl had just explained that Bathandwa preferred to speak English.

'Yes,' said Bathandwa, smiling.

'Okay, good, what is the name of this place we are in, do you know?'

'I don't know,' said Bathandwa.

'Do you know what day it is?' asked Sister K.

'Saturday,' said Bathandwa. I had to think for a second before I realised it was Thursday.

'And the year?' said Sister K, unconcerned. Bathandwa frowned.

'Can't remember?' said Sister K after a pause.

'Can't remember,' she mumbled.

'And the month?' asked Sister.

Bathandwa paused. 'December,' she said. It was February.

'Where do you live?' asked Sister K.

'In the convent,' said Bathandwa.

'In the convent?' Sister K glanced at the daughter, who said something in Xhosa.

'I see,' said Sister K. 'Who do you live with?'

'Other little girls,' said Bathandwa, and she giggled. Sister K said something else to the family and the daughter shook her head.

'Have you ever used alcohol?' Sister K asked. Bathandwa smiled guiltily. She was a child again, being admonished.

'Yes,' she said.

'And what do you think this building is? Do you think this is a police station or a hospital?' I wondered why she had chosen those two options. But then, what else could a room like this be? Bathandwa said something I couldn't understand.

'Hospital? You are a smart one, eh?' said Sister K.

Soon Bathandwa and her family were sent away and new patients were called in, often in family groups, and sometimes alone, and those ones I think sometimes looked afraid to be there alone. They spoke softly, the way people speak in prayer. My mind began to wander again after the brief thrill of being able to understand something.

At some point, two women were there, an older woman and, perhaps, her daughter. Sister K asked the older woman something and she didn't answer, but swallowed, clutched her throat, and shook her head.

'She can speak, but when she go to speak there is a poison,' said the daughter, inexplicably in English. 'She can taste poison.' Then she returned to speaking Xhosa.

I had not eaten anything that day—I had missed my chance to drop by the coffee shop before the van arrived to pick me up, and I could feel myself drifting to sleep in my seat. Every few seconds, I found myself falling forward and jerked awake again. I tried to focus on the page in front of me. I took my pen and wrote *coffee coffee coffee coffee*. If I kept writing, it would be impossible to fall asleep, I thought, but my eyes were struggling to focus. The words on the page began to look more like *crrrrghh*, like some internal mechanism grinding to a halt. I tried to listen and guess what was being said. It seemed like you could understand it, if you just listened hard enough.

The day before, a patient had spoken to me. It was the only time someone had really spoken to me here. There was a large girl in a pink jumpsuit, an older woman in a purple and yellow jumpsuit, and the patient. You could always tell who the patient was when they had relatives with them, because they were the only one not speaking to Sister K.

He was a boy, late teens maybe, and he was looking directly at me. He started talking to me in Xhosa, and they all stopped to watch.

'I don't speak Xhosa,' I said. 'Sorry.'

He didn't stop speaking, though. He was staring at me intently. I looked around for help but Sister K was just watching calmly.

'I don't speak Xhosa.'

'You speak English, eh?'

'Yes,' I said.

'What's your number?' he said, grinning.

'I don't think that's appropriate,' I said. He kept talking in Xhosa, faster and faster, his eyes fixed, white, glaring.

'I don't understand,' I tried to say.

He switched back to English. 'You have a boyfriend?'

'Yes,' I lied.

'Where do you live? Where you staying?'

'I can't tell you that.' He talked at me in Xhosa again, faster and louder, he was smiling but it was not a friendly smile, his nose wrinkling, his stare fixed. 'What's he saying?' I asked Sister K, but she did not reply, just watched in silence. He kept on like that for a few minutes before abruptly returning to English.

'See here,' he said. 'I'm going to come to your house where you live, I'm going to kill your boyfriend and I'm going to fuck you. I'm going to fuck you and I'm going to kill you.'

Sister K and the two family members looked bored.

'You hear me?' the boy said. 'I'm going to fuck you until you're dead.'

The girl in the pink jumpsuit laughed. 'Don't worry,' she said. 'He's just crazy.'

'Lunchtime,' said Sister K to me, when the next patient left. I had forgotten to bring my lunch.

'Do you know if there is anywhere I can buy food?' I asked.

'Not in here. This is a hospital,' said Sister K.

'Right.' I had been imagining a little cafeteria with a gift shop hidden in some corner of this maze of corridors, but of course that would be ridiculous here. 'There's nowhere nearby?'

'Of course, anywhere, they are lined up against that wall. There are stalls everywhere,' she said, picking up her handbag and a pile of paperwork, gesturing at me to leave so she could lock the room.

I made my way past the waiting people, out the way I had entered and into the car park, a fenced area of sand and tarseal and piss-stagnant air. If I didn't eat, I would faint. The entrance to the car park was guarded by two security guards in uniform. Beyond that, there must be street stalls, as Sister K had said, selling all kinds of food. I had seen some of them on the drive here. Meat roasting over spits, and bowls of 'papas and beans'. But I was surprised that Sister K would suggest I leave the compound. I had been led to believe it was dangerous.

I walked the length of the car park, nodded to the guards, who nodded and said, 'Molo, afternoon, ma'am,' looking amused maybe, because I shouldn't be out here alone, or maybe they did not look amused but were just smiling politely.

I was out on the road. It looked larger and emptier than it had on the way here. There were a few wall-less, tent-like structures against a large industrial building. It looked like those tents could be selling something, but there were no signs, no outward-facing counters. There were people in the tents, standing around in circles. In another context, they could have been families setting up camp at a festival. A woman squatting against the wall of the large building was watching me, so I picked a direction and made my way around one side of the building. There was a wide entrance. It looked like a mall. There were signs indicating the shops inside, and one of them said 'Hungry Lion'. As soon as I entered the building I began to map my distance from the security guards, in my head. The walls made it feel so much further away. I thought about that boy who had promised to rape and kill me. I'd read on the internet that you shouldn't go to a township like Khayelitsha, especially if you are white, unless you are on a guided tour, as it is very dangerous. Any foreigner would stand out as a target, and the police didn't always have a lot of access in the townships. And perhaps it was true—there must have been a reason for the guards outside the hospital grounds. But it was hard to tell how much of that advice was just fear-mongering, or tourists relaying the same advice that they'd received without questioning it.

There were a few people in the building—a mother with a young child, and a cleaner. Both the woman and the child watched me out of the corners of their eyes as they continued walking. The only place that looked open was the Hungry Lion, a greasy little takeaway chicken shop with a bright yellow and red menu behind the counter. It looked a bit like a KFC.

'Hi,' I said. The woman at the counter chewed her gum, watching me with curiosity. The voices from the kitchen went quiet.

I looked at the menu. It was written partly in Xhosa or Zulu or Afrikaans, or maybe it was just the stress that made my eyes jump to words I didn't recognise, but I managed to pick out the word 'chicken' somewhere and repeated the title. She repeated it back, and I said, 'Yes, please.'

I glanced at my phone. I had about seven minutes. I sat down on a red bench and looked at my phone again in the hope that it would slow time down. The soles of my sandals were peeling apart. I pressed the two flaps apart against the ground. A couple of kids and two women in yoga pants holding bags of shopping to their bellies entered the mall and looked in at the Hungry Lion, laughing. I couldn't hear them through the glass.

'Lady?' said the woman working the till. She held out a large Hungry Chicken bucket in a plastic bag. I looked inside. It was filled with chicken drumsticks. Was that really what I had ordered? I looked at my watch. Two minutes.

'Enkosi,' I said, and grabbed the bag. I would have to bring this bucket into the psychiatric office. The bag was transparent and only just big enough, so you could see the Hungry Chicken logo through the plastic. I tried to hold it closed at the top, but it wouldn't close. I speed-walked back to the hospital compound, past the security guards, and towards the door. I didn't want Sister K to think I was lazy, and some part of me was still hoping that this internship could be salvaged, that if I built up some trust, she might translate things now and then for me, so that I might learn something that would make all of this worthwhile—something about the way she spoke or the questions she asked or how she always seemed to have an answer that would make the patient nod and say 'Enkosi,

Sister', as if assured that they had indeed been sent to the right place, that they were in good hands. But I had to eat. There was no way I could eat in that room.

Behind a tree, I leaned against the side of the building and bit into a piece of chicken. I could feel the greasy spiciness being transformed into energy and entering my bloodstream. My fingers dripped with fat. I threw the bones in the dirt and wiped my lips, tried to wipe my fingers against the side of the box, and stepped into the corridor, holding the chicken bucket low under my arm as if it didn't exist. You could smell it in the corridor immediately. The rich, deep-fried, chicken-in-spicy-batter smell was impossible to mistake. As I walked down the corridor past the waiting areas and more corridors, people lined against the walls looked at me with my chicken, and they all looked at the chicken. Only I did not look at the chicken. I kept walking and not looking at the chicken, all the way to room 26, where Sister K saw my bundle and gave the new patient a look that I interpreted to mean 'Tch, these Americans'. I stuffed the chicken into the cabinet and sat down, saying, 'Molo, Molweni' and 'Enkosi', which meant thank you, because I didn't know how to say sorry. But it was no good. The smell permeated everything.

Wo(und)man

'I think there is something wrong with me,' said the woman.

'What seems to be the problem?' asked the doctor.

'Well,' she said, 'I am so tired, all the time, I feel as though I am losing blood. I am turning blue and my veins have started showing themselves all over like neon street signs in a foreign language, and . . .'

She paused in discomfort, but the doctor said nothing and waited for her to continue.

'And, you have to understand, there is a great gold dagger in my chest with a hilt like a serpent, and a sword in my stomach. I can feel it ripping me apart when I move and eat, and when I lie awake in bed at night.'

'Would you say you have trouble sleeping?' asked the doctor.

'Yes,' said the woman.

'And this pain,' said the doctor, 'could you number it on a scale with ten being similar to the experience of giving birth to quintuplets on horseback, and one being a mere annoyance (as in you shouldn't even be here at all, you time waster, you cowardly woman)?'

'Five?' said the woman tentatively. She did not want to complain.

'Very well,' said the doctor, 'can you tick the relevant boxes in this list?'

The woman tried to look at the lists and tick the right boxes, but after a while she began to think she was just imagining her illness after all, because none of the things on the list seemed exactly right, although they all seemed about half right as if they described a televised version of her whose illness interrupted a life more healthy and well-arranged than her own, full of work functions and functional relationships where anything out of place could be noticed and marked down as disease.

'Do you think it's just depression?' the woman asked.

'Do you think it is?' said the doctor.

'It could be,' said the woman. 'Sometimes I don't know if I am tired or sad. Sometimes I don't know if I am imagining things.'

'Very well,' said the doctor, 'there are some pills you can take.'

The woman hesitated. 'Are you sure?'

'Well'—the doctor shrugged—'it's like we always say, if you feel bad, why not? There's no harm in trying.'

The woman assented and went home to swallow her first pill with a glass of water. The next day, new pains began. She realised that there was a spear in her foot, and then two arrows in her thigh, and soon she had a dull ache from a club to the shoulder. Her skin began to tighten, her fingers and toes going numb and stiff.

All night she listened to her heart. It went *crrrrrrrr* and then began beating in 3/4 like a waltz and then for a long time she was sure it did not beat at all. The dagger was still wedged into her left atrium. The hilt with its gilded serpent seemed to leer up at her. She waited for a heart attack and considered calling for help. But how silly she would look if it were not a heart attack. Instead she wrote a short note to her family, apologising for not having called for help, so that they would not resent her so much when they found her body and realised how cowardly she had been.

She realised then that her hands had been replaced by someone else's hands. They were pale, much skinnier, and clammy, as though they had been stored in a jar for many years. They moved only in stiff jerks that seemed just a little detached from her intentions, as though someone else were manipulating her hands in a way that was meant to convince her she was still in control of them. She began to develop suspicions.

The following day she was a little better and had gotten used to the spears and arrows and even the dagger. But the sword in her stomach was unsettling, and she could not think of eating.

She swam in the ocean and became the ocean, feeling no joy, the water sliding in and out of her brain. And she began to feel the brain behind her cheeks turn to statue. The once fertile breeding grounds for new and surprising thoughts were now fossilised.

She could not do maths anymore. She returned to the doctor and told him that she had taken an IQ test and had dropped twenty points. She told him about her hands being wrong, about the spears and arrows which she could not remove. But she did not tell him about her heart, or the note she had hidden, crumpled into a fist beneath the rotting banana peels.

'Well,' said the doctor, 'it was you who called it depression, don't you recall?'

The woman went home again on the bus. She still had the dagger in her heart, the spear in her foot, the arrows in her thigh, and the sword in her stomach. She bled onto the floor of the bus and this made her tired. On the bus too was a woman with an axe in her brain, wedged in neatly as you would wedge it into a block of wood while it wasn't in use. On the other side of the bus, another woman had her stomach cut open and her baby was sitting across from her, still attached to its umbilical cord, crying and waving its little pink arms. That heartless woman did nothing to comfort her baby, just stared at it, unaffected, as the poor thing ruined everyone's bus ride with its bawling. Everywhere was blood, drying into the seats, the dank sweet rust smell permeating everything, and she couldn't even read the paper.

Bloodhounds

The yellow flag in the entrance to our marquee said 'Unit 7: Hibis-kisses', but it was sopping wet and twisting up in the wind so that you couldn't read it. I wondered, if I could float up into the storm, how many white marquees I would see scattered across the grass like knucklebones, and how many army-green tents. There were 2999 other twelve-year-old girl guides at Jamboree, and I didn't know any of them. I'd travelled six hours to this place by bus with forty other hibis-kisses, and when we arrived everything was torrential. Tents collapsed as we put them up. One of them lifted off the ground and tried to roly-poly away. It felt so long since morning I thought I might fall asleep standing.

We were supposed to sort ourselves into tent groups while we were setting up. The other girls had been making secret pacts all afternoon with their own friends, and I didn't know how to ask about being in their groups. I was supposed to be doing something to help, but I wasn't sure exactly what. I just stood there, the rain crawling through my hair. I could have been waist deep in wet concrete. I was watching two girls who wore yellow mesh skirts that shrouded their track pants to match the droopy flag. One was waving a mallet around and the other was bent over, counting pegs and flinging them with a *ting* onto a silver pile.

I was going to ask Carmen first, but she was busy talking to the other girls. Vanessa, the girl I'd sat next to on the bus, said she was the nicest. 'Carmen's funny and she gives us Mackintoshes sometimes,' she'd said, pointing her out. Carmen had long, horse-brown hair. One of the other leaders was supposedly the mean one you had to watch out for, but I couldn't remember which one. I shivered. The wind was wet and pulling back the hood of my rain jacket and the sky seemed much larger than normal. When I stared up at the rain, it seemed the sky was constantly expanding, grey clouds being pulled apart into individual rain drops over and over. I stood there with my fists shoved in my wet jacket pockets and wished that I had chickened out in the beginning and not come.

'What are you standing about for, love? Are you looking for something to do?' One of the guide leaders was squinting at me, frowning, a red crate hanging disassembled and gaping from her hand. I figured she could be the grumpy one, as she didn't smile when she spoke like the others did. She was older, with wrinkles that cut down the middle of her forehead like exclamation points.

'Sorry,' I said. 'It's just . . .'

'What's that, hon? My hearing's not the best.'

'I don't have a tent,' I said. 'I don't really, I mean, there's no one from my unit.'

'Well, that's all right. That's what Jamboree's all about, meeting new people.' She stomped into the marquee and dropped the crate on the grass. 'Eleanor,' she said, and a girl stopped on her way out of the tent. She carried another red crate in her arms and had just the same expression as the guide leader. 'How many do you have in your tent?'

'Uh, five, I think,' said Eleanor.

'Room for one more, then. You could fit Madison in, right?'

'Sure.'

'Oh, Maddy, Maddy, come with us,' said Vanessa, who had just sidled up to the guide leader, holding a bent tent-pole and pushing her glasses back into her waterlogged hair. 'Bev, we have an extra space too, can she come with us?'

'Up to her. There you go, hon,' said Bev, turning back to me. 'You're popular now.'

'Pick us, pick us,' said another girl, pointing enthusiastically at herself and Vanessa. Her dark hair was stuck down with a tie-dyed scarf and randomly placed clips.

'I'm Emily,' she said. So I said I guess I'd pick them, and Vanessa gave the pole to Bev and they both squealed. 'Our tent is the best,' said Emily, 'even though they're all the same. Come see anyway.' And they leaped off across the grass, stomping in the puddles. I leaped after them. Suddenly I wasn't tired anymore, none of us were; we almost could have leapfrogged right over those tents.

*

The rain stopped in the morning, and after we'd had breakfast in the marquee and washed our plates in buckets by the door, we could explore. The three of us linked arms: Vanessa in the middle with me and Emily on either side.

'Slow down,' whined Emily to Vanessa, who was bounding towards a grassy intersection.

'I need to finish my toast,' I added, through a mouthful. Vanessa tried to pull us ahead, and Emily and I, giving our slyest looks to each other over Vanessa's shoulder to signal that each of us knew what the other was thinking, both began to lean backwards, allowing ourselves to be pulled along, our feet sliding in the wet grass like water-skis. 'Come on, my two whining children,' said Vanessa, digging her heels in.

We passed other units identical to ours, each with rows of green tents and a white marquee with people lining up to wash dishes outside the door. In the distance there were more marquees clustered around a barn which stuck out above the white canvas roofs like a haunted mansion in an otherwise pristine suburb. As it heated up, the damp grass emitted a whiff of cow dung, and there was a smell of musty tents airing out, and milk-logged cornflakes, and dish soap.

We turned onto a gravel road where many people had converged and were also walking towards the barn. The tents were further apart, and there were rides and games: a giant chess set, and a sheep dip with a girl in togs sitting metres above it on a chair. The chair was dropped down on a big wooden lever, and the girl was plunged squealing into the pool, her eyes scrunched up and her fists stiff at her sides as if to punch the water. The crowd around her laughed.

Next to the barn itself were two trampolines with massive

crane-like structures above them holding bungee cords to which people were strapped.

'It's like a trampoline bungee,' said Vanessa.

'It looks like one of those jolly jumper things for babies!' I said. I remembered how as a toddler I'd been very upset when I grew out of my jolly jumper.

By the time we reached the front of the line, the crowds were loud and the sun had driven all the damp out of the grass. I could smell the hairspray of the girl ahead of me, but if I tried to face away from it there were people pushing past in twos and threes; there wasn't anywhere left to look without accidentally staring at someone.

Then it was my turn on the trampoline. I was jumping higher than the force of my legs and I could see all the rides and the people in their blue-green guide shirts. Though the crowd had seemed stifling from the ground, I could now see that it was concentrated in the immediate vicinity of the barn. Beyond it, there was clear space and grass which nobody seemed to want.

'Maddy.' Down below Emily was pointing the camera. 'Say cheese.' I flung my legs and arms out wide and grinned. I wished I could stay in the air.

By the time we'd all had a go on the trampolines, the best rides had long lines. It was hot and windless, the kind of weather that is usually reserved for school athletics days. We wandered towards the nearby marquees, which held the lesser craft activities that you could do when you had finished all the good stuff.

The first one we came to had a line out the doorway. There were trestle tables inside, each with a little tray of craft materials and a different unit leader holding the station, so you went from one station to the next like you were on a conveyer belt. The first tray was full of black string.

'Take a piece of string,' said the woman, yawning. 'Pardon me,' she added, covering her mouth, but I didn't think that it was her fault for being tired of standing in a tent handing out string. The second tray held little pieces of pāua shell with holes drilled in them.

'Pick one you like,' said another woman, pushing the tray towards me. I picked out a piece of pāua, one of the few left that had colour in them.

Next was a thin smiling woman with a forehead lined like a musical stave. 'Now, this is how you thread the shell so that it stays in the centre.' She demonstrated with her own, threading it and making a little loop so it held on neatly from the top. 'There you are, you're a pro,' she said when I copied her. 'Now go and see Neve over there.'

I followed to where she pointed, to a woman with long blond hair in a plait. 'Hello!' she said. 'What's your full name?'

When I told her, she grabbed a stack of laminated things marked 'H' from a box and flicked through them. 'Ah! Here you are. Madison Ruth Hamill.'

She handed me a bookmark, with my name printed on it, followed by the words 'You Are Special' and a poem underneath.

You are special
And nobody could take your place

No one else has your fingerprints

91

No one else has your palm prints
No one else has your footprints

There is no one else
Who can say a word
Exactly the way you do.
No one can say 'Buffalo'
Exactly like you do

Scientists also tell us that
No one smells the same way you do.
That's why bloodhound dogs can
find people after smelling their clothing

It went on like that. I guessed I was supposed to be relieved that bloodhound dogs could find me so easily, but I'd never been afraid that I blended in too much. It struck me as a strange thing to worry about. Most people, you would think, would prefer not to be *that* special.

'Now,' said Neve, 'can I tie your necklace?'

I moved my hair out of the way and she held the necklace on me, getting it the right length, and then she tied it in a knot, explaining all the time how each piece of shell or stone was different and special. Vanessa and Emily came out after me, so I waited for them.

'I bet a really good movie actor could say buffalo the way I do, if they were playing me in a movie,' I said.

'Bet I can say buffalo the same as you,' Vanessa said.

'Buffalo,' I said.

'Buffalo,' she said back.

'It is, it's exactly the same!' said Emily. I laughed. 'Do me, do me,' said Emily. 'Buffalo.'

'Do me, do me, buffalo,' said Vanessa after her.

'Oh my gosh, help me! I'm having an identity crisis! I'm not special,' said Emily.

'You're nuts,' said Vanessa. 'Come on, let's go to lunch.'

'I need to pee,' I said. 'I'll see you there.'

There was a line of portaloos near us. I picked the one that looked the cleanest, where the smell of urine was not so overwhelming. Everything inside had a teal-coloured light, and I only glanced down at my new yellow underwear when it came time to pull it up, and I thought for a second that I had a blind spot in my eye, but it wasn't—it was the undies. A dark blood stain the size of my hand. I sat back down again.

My first thought was that I didn't know that it would be so dark like that. And my second thought was, why now? Why, of all possible times, would it have to be now, at this camp in this hot, green portaloo?

I didn't cry because there would have been no use. I tried to imagine what one of those cooler girls in my primary school class would do. Coolness, it seemed to me, was really an elite kind of ordinariness, like bottled mineral water. Take Greer Thomlinson, for example. Greer was someone I didn't know very well but when I tried to think what an 'ordinary' girl would do, I imagined Greer. When Greer had her hair plaited, there was never a strand out of place. It was all lined up, stronger and straighter than normal hair, like the hair on a Barbie doll. It was true she had a bit of a funny name, and her mother smoked out the car window, but she had an ordinary kind of house with a trampoline and a Hungry Hippos game, and it was very tidy, like the houses on television, and all her things looked new. I bet if Greer were in my situation, she would go straight to Bev, who was the counsellor and first-aid person for our unit as well as a leader, and explain what had happened, and maybe she would cry a little and then Bev would give her everything she needed, and Greer would call her mum and her mum would say something encouraging and then everything would carry on as usual.

My own mum might have offered similarly encouraging advice, as that was a sort of requirement for parents, but I thought I could make up the advice just as well in my head anyway, so I might as well not bother her. Then I realised that actually I was supposed to have brought supplies for this happening; it had been in the list of things to bring, along with three different kinds of shoes and ten hundred jumpers and mittens and sunglasses and a first-aid kit. It had been on the list for everyone, just in case you got your first period at camp. I felt that horrible emptiness of having forgotten something and never being able to un-forget it. Bev probably wouldn't have supplies for this if we were supposed to bring them, and she might be grumpy that I hadn't come prepared, and she might then feel like she had to give me her own supplies, or maybe she'd be too old and wouldn't have them anymore, or she would have to buy me some, and it would be a whole thing, and everyone would find out.

If I never left this portaloo, everything would be fine. I thought this for a while, and the smell of the portaloo started to become unnoticeable, until abruptly I knew that I couldn't stay in the portaloo any longer.

I pulled out a bunch of toilet paper and tried to stick it

inside my undies but it just unscrunched itself. What if it fell out? I was starting to panic. Then I had an idea.

I unrolled a lot of toilet paper from the roll and wound it around the bloody part of my underwear to make a pad. It seemed to stick okay, although it was the thin, cheap toilet paper so it probably wouldn't last long. I pulled my pants up and washed my hands. Then I stepped outside. My eyes went staticky for a second, readjusting.

When I got back to our camp, everyone was in the marquee having lunch. I could hear the clatter of plates and cups, and everyone talking at once in there. It was strange being outside of the noise, like listening to the kids' wave pool after you've stepped outside and the water has popped and run out of your ears. I wanted to go in, but instead I went to the tent and found a new pair of underwear and put it in my pocket with the pocket money I had brought with me in case of an emergency. I had five dollars. I zipped the tent behind me and went back down the now empty path towards the barn.

The barn was a dark and dusty space, and even bigger now that there was nothing going on. So tall you'd wonder if it was technically the sky up in the roof. It reminded me of the guy from the bible who had too much grain so he built bigger barns and then God made him die just to teach him a lesson about greed. At the back of the barn, in a dust-dull corner, was a woman at a trestle table selling first-aid things and necessities like hats and sunscreen, and branded rain jackets. She was wearing a wide-brimmed sunhat, like she had turned up to the beach in the wrong weather. The tampons and pads were laid out, one of each kind, on one corner of her trestle table.

I could afford a larger eight-pack of tampons, or a small six-pack of pads. The pads were the thinner ones, and probably the wrong kind. Everything else was seven or eight dollars. The tampons freaked me out a little. What if I couldn't figure them out? Then they'd be no use, and anyway, it was weird and gross to put those things up there. Also, some of the boxes were longer and said 'with applicator'. Did you need an applicator to apply them?

'Do you need help?' asked the woman.

'Um, I'll just get these ones,' I said, pointing to the pads, and trying not to speak too loudly, so the girl browsing nearby couldn't hear. Then I knew I had made a mistake, because six pads were only, I guessed, three days' worth at the most, and what was I going to do for the remaining three days of camp? Maybe it would have stopped by then. I couldn't remember if periods lasted only a couple of days or if it was more like a week.

Every few hours there was more blood, and I had a pain all through the trip to the science museum the next day. I imagined it was sort of like a ripe passionfruit up in there, and its insides had been scraped out with a spoon, and I could feel them dripping. I tried to look at the tuatara egg, the drawers of little bugs with so much writing about them, and the coloured liquids that floated in the glass things. It got better later, when we went to the Antarctic Centre, and it wasn't even so bad when we rode in the Hägglund truck, which drove through snow and slush, bumping us all over the place with the grey silt water running over the windows as if we were being buried. Everyone but me screamed.

The next morning, I had no pads left. I went into the portaloo and wound the toilet paper around my underwear again. The only problem was that when it was too quiet, I could hear the paper rustle. Also, I couldn't bend over too much, or jump around uncontrollably, or do the splits.

I became slow and ladylike. When Vanessa tried to run fast, dragging me and Emily after her, I really had to insist on floating along slowly, as if in a whimsical mood, looking up at the sky, which was as clean as a new blue rain jacket. We went to the zoo, and a siamang gibbon poked its fingers through the wires and looked right into me with her black eyes. I hated it when the others started taking pictures of her. I knew the gibbon didn't really want to be photographed. Carmen said she wanted food but we shouldn't give her anything. I thought she just looked sad and maybe she knew that I was a bit sad too. I imagined that the gibbon and I understood each other, that she was telepathically imparting to me a primal secret. But I knew that it was unlikely she would have picked me out. Maybe this was a trick for food. Maybe there were a hundred other people before me who had made eye contact with the gibbon and imagined they were the chosen one, receiving primal wisdom, which you can't understand but you can feel; you can feel yourself growing older and wiser by the second.

Whenever no one was looking, I twisted around to check my pants and wondered how I looked and whether you could smell it. The smell was something that bothered me more and more. I wondered if they had bloodhounds at the zoo. I sat with my legs closed, and I tried to test-smell the air around me from time to time, but I had become immune to it, and sometimes I caught a whiff of something sweet and clingy and soiled and I wondered if it was me, or if it was because we had just passed the loos. But the more I became aware of the smell, the more I thought I smelled it in the strangest of places, and it wasn't coming from me, because I could put my head to my knees and smell again, and it wouldn't get any stronger. It was a smell out there in the world, or in my mind, maybe.

The blood kept going on and on, and I ached all the time, an ache like you think the wind is feeling when it howls against the windows. The ache made me sit up straight; it was not the sort of feeling you could slump into. I looked at my reflection in the side of the glass building as we waited for the bus back to camp. My back was huddled forward and I tried to straighten it and put my shoulders back, in that way that women do because the pain deep down makes them endure, and to endure means to stand up straight so as to carry this bleeding wound inside of you like it's an expensive vase.

Whatever I did, the blood always soaked around the sides of the toilet paper and left dark stains on my undies. I put them in the plastic bag I had brought for my laundry and folded it up tight. Every time I opened the bag to put a new pair in, it stank. I was running out of underwear too, and I worried that it would all be permanently stained or go mouldy and I would have to explain to Mum why all my underwear was ruined because I hadn't gone to Bev straight away like anyone with half a brain would have. But I couldn't go to Bev now. I would have to explain why I hadn't told anyone before.

On the second to last day of Jamboree, during dinner when everyone else was still eating, I took the plastic bag out of my tent and took it to the tap that ran outside the lunch tent, with a cake of soap in an ice-cream pottle underneath. Bev and Carmen and a group of other unit leaders were sitting a few metres away, but I didn't think they would notice me. I peeped at them from time to time, out of the corner of my eye, in case anyone should get any closer. There was a small tree next to the tap, which gave a little bit of cover.

There was a particularly good sunset going on, with a pinkish glow, and everything had extra texture because of the shadows; you could see every blade of grass. I took the undies out in a big bunch and put them under the water and squeezed. The water ran red into the dirt. I kept running the water and squeezing and the water kept running red, and I began to realise what a stupid idea it was, because there was no way I could dry them all and now they would be wet in the bag, but it was too late. I got the soap and tried to rub some through and then I rinsed and rinsed, but it never stopped. Red water ran down through the wooden slats of the platform, some into the drain, and the rest sinking into the dirt. People started to come out of the tent to wash their dishes in the crates of washing water, and I began to panic. My hands were getting tired, and I squeezed the soaking bundle one more time, put it back in the plastic bag and carried it quickly back to my tent. I took one pair out and left them to dry on the guy ropes next to an old T-shirt, and I left the rest in the plastic bag. I didn't touch it again, just left it hidden under the spare shoes in my bag, a big coiled glob sweating in the plastic.

That night everyone from the Hibis-kisses unit had to go to the barn, and several other units were there so it was a crowd. There was a jumpy sort of music playing on the loudspeaker, and a woman on a megaphone.

'You should all have a slip of paper at the back of your Jamboree booklets. There's space there for a lot of names. I want you all to meet as many new people as possible. Don't be shy. The person who fills up their sheet first might win a prize.'

The music was put up loud again, and everyone started moving and talking to one another.

A girl approached me. 'Hi.' She had a tiny little mouth, and she smiled apologetically so her lips disappeared into her freckles. 'I'm Jenna.'

'I'm Maddy,' I said. I uncrossed my arms so as not to look hostile. 'Where are you from?'

'Cromwell,' said Jenna.

'With the giant fruit?' I remembered driving past the giant plastic pear, apricot and apple stuck up on poles with the sign for Cromwell.

'Yeah.'

'Okay,' I said, since that was all I knew about Cromwell. 'I'm from Dunedin.'

'Nice to meet you,' said Jenna from Cromwell. We swapped booklets and I signed my name and unit.

'Thanks,' she said, and went away.

'Maddy. Sign mine,' said Vanessa.

'Okay,' I said, taking the booklet. 'Where's Emily?'

'She's taking some time out.' Vanessa pointed, and I saw Emily sitting alone against the wall at the far end of the barn, cross-legged as if she were meditating.

I wandered down towards Emily. The crowd looked small from all the way at the other side of the barn. The roof was so high above and the floor so large that the crowd had stuck mostly to the one corner where the loudspeakers were. Here, the music was much less thumpy.

'Hi, can I join you?' I asked. She nodded, so I sat down next to her.

It was beautiful there with our backs to the wall, watching all the people in blue-green jerseys babbling in the distance like a penguin colony, and stars just showing in the sky at the end of the barn roof, and the big tall stage lights lighting everything as if it were the stage for a Broadway musical.

'I can't possibly meet any more people today,' said Emily.

'Me neither,' I said.

On the last day, the underwear I had left on the guy rope was partially dry, so I wrapped it extra securely in the toilet paper. Luckily the blood was much less by then, so it was okay. I didn't have to check it so much. In the evening, there was a huge concert with Evermore, Spacifix and Elemeno P, and all three thousand girls at the Jamboree were there. I felt wide awake by then, packed in the hall with everyone in our identical blue-green T-shirts, the drumbeat thudding through us. People began jumping up and down and waving their arms. For the first time in my life, I wasn't uncomfortable to be in a crowd, and I jumped up and down and waved my fist too and let the music pulse through me, and I didn't care that it hurt my ears and the flashing lights were making me blind. I didn't care about anything at all. Confetti exploded over our heads and we all jumped and tried to catch it. I caught some and put it in my pockets, red and blue and green and gold stars.

Afterwards, we walked in double file back to camp. I hung back at the end of the line. Everyone was excited and chattering. I felt as if my head with its bright red hair was bobbing obscenely above the rest of them like a helium balloon, and I wondered if I should look down and check if any blood had leaked during all the headbanging.

'Hi Maddy,' said Carmen, slowing so that she came in

beside me. 'Did you enjoy the concert?'

'Yes, it was fun.'

'How old are you, Maddy?'

'I'm twelve,' I said.

'Really? You know what, you look like you could be sixteen,' said Carmen.

'Really?' I said.

'Yes. I suppose you seem more mature because you're so quiet.'

I smiled. It was dark, and the streetlights were growing further apart as we made our way back towards the campsite, which shone through the trees in bumblebee stripes. I walked with my back straight like a ballerina and my legs just as graceful, without a sound.

Specimen

We had never thought to question why our school would own a preserved tapeworm before that day in Year 11. We'd just sort of thought that all schools kept one in their science corridor, like a trophy. Maybe they did. It had just now occurred to us that there was something a bit weird about that.

'Like, where did they get the tapeworm?'

'Maybe Mrs Swan got infected with tapeworms and donated it,' said Liv. She bit the corner of her Juicie, crushing the ice with her teeth before she sucked it out of the little plastic sleeve.

'You know you have to, like, pull them out of your anus or they kill you,' I said.

'I don't think that's true.' Liv peered at the coiled flat white worm in its jar at the back of the glass cabinet. 'I don't think it would be strong enough to survive being pulled out of an anus.'

I shivered. 'Why would she donate her tapeworm to the school display cabinet?'

'For science,' said Liv.

Now that the school owned it, it was a communal tapeworm. I wondered if the school could sell it as a movie prop and save up for a baritone saxophone.

'Who decides when the school sells things?' I asked.

'The Board of Trustees. Haley's mum is one of them.'

'So, it's Haley's mum's tapeworm?' I said.

'Yes, Maddy. It's Haley's mum's tapeworm.' I'd noticed Liv had developed a way of responding to my questions that made her sound like the parent of a small child.

'Why did we come early to science class, Liv?' I said, lying down. The door to the class was locked during lunch, so we were shut out in the corridor.

'Because we're lame and can't manage our time. What are you doing?'

'Having a nap.' I was so tired, and so restless. I always seemed to be that way. I lay starfished on the cold, scuffed floor and listened to the shudder of footsteps passing us on the main corridor, which intersected this one a couple of metres behind my head. The sun was shining in lemonade swatches on the linoleum. The air and light above me had a rising quality, as if I could float up into it at any moment.

At school we had to entertain ourselves a lot, while they made us wait for this or that learning experience. There was always another badly written assessment or educational game or survey or careers aptitude test or motivational speech— the logical inconsistencies of which we were not encouraged to criticise—and more time waiting for the bell to ring, for the roll to be called, for the others to shut up, for ourselves to shut up, for yesterday's lesson to be repeated. It was kind of okay in our small group with its jokes and games. It was like I'd commandeered a lifeboat with my friends as captives. If we took turns to keep inflating it as we went along, we wouldn't drown.

I rolled onto my side and peered into the dusty cabinet. I had never looked closely at the bottom shelf. There was something that looked like a roll of old wallpaper under a film of soft grey dust, like mouse fur. And there were a couple of other jars with what could have been intestines inside them. Behind them was something that looked like it was sleeping.

I held my breath when I saw him, his little sleeping face, with the soft drawn-back ears, his perfect furless elephant-grey body, curled into himself. I could just see, in the shadows, his tiny, newly formed cloven hooves, drifting in the jar as if in a womb.

Once, our English teacher, Dr Barringer, showed us *American Beauty*. She was explaining how a plastic bag or a severed head could be beautiful. The movie ends with someone being murdered, and the person who finds the body gazes at it in wonder. Dr Barringer said she often thought that something sad and gruesome could be beautiful, like a dead bird for instance.

'Do you not think a dead bird is beautiful? Anyone? Raise your hand,' she said. Nobody raised their hand, and she seemed sad. Then someone said, 'Nah, Miss. Beautiful is, like, good stuff. Cause death and shit is like, ugly you know.'

Everyone was like, 'Yeah.' But secretly, I agreed with Dr Barringer.

'Is it a lamb, do you think?' I asked Liv.

'I don't know. He looks sort of goat-like,' she said. She was right—he had long pointy ears folding in on themselves at the tips.

'I bet he's a goat,' I said. 'Goats go to hell in *Godspell*.' It was the musical the school was putting on that year. 'The sheep go to heaven, and the goats go to hell.'

'What? Why?'

'Because sheep are privileged little arseholes who can't think for themselves. It's a cruel world. My poor baby goat.' I sighed. 'You know I've always wanted to adopt.'

'You adopt the goat and I'll adopt the tapeworm.'

'You can come in now,' said Mrs Swan. She was a buck-toothed wiry woman with a wild pixie cut and a hint of helium in her voice. She was a nice teacher who didn't monologue when she was upset.

'Maddy, you can come back and look at the baby goat after,' Liv said, holding out a hand. I made Liv act like my mother sometimes. The more bored I was, the more my brain started to get like a toddler, attaching itself to passing objects. But I went to class and I even started doing the worksheets about Mendel and his peas with their dominant and recessive genes, making them different sizes and shapes in a sort of times-tables grid that you had to keep drawing over and over.

'Miss,' I said when she was on her way down the aisle. 'Can we see the dead things in the jars?'

'What, sorry?'

'The ones in the cabinet. Please can we take them out?'

'Oh, you mean the specimens.'

The specimens!

'I'll tell you what, if you two get your work done today, I'll take them out for you to look at.'

We really did get our work done quietly after that, me because I really wanted to see the specimens and Liv because she actually liked science and I wasn't distracting her.

So Mrs Swan went out to unlock the cabinet and started setting the jars up at the front of the class. There was a baby rat still attached to its umbilical cord. There was the brain of a small mammal, a seventies-patterned frog, and the tapeworm which, it turned out, had been retrieved from a euthanised horse.

And, of course, the goat. I held it in my hands. The jar was kind of warm. The little hooves looked as soft as my own toes. 'Is he a goat, Miss?'

'Yes, that's a male goat foetus. Would have been a still birth.' A still birth, like a still life.

The goat's face was serene. His skin was wrinkly, like fingers after a hot bath. He would never have opened his eyes or breathed. The umbilical cord still extruded from his little belly and wound around his body like a scarf.

'Can I keep him, Miss?' I asked.

'No.'

'But I love him.'

'Maddy,' she said, in a warning tone.

'I'll give him a good home.'

'No.'

For a while, every time we passed the turn-off to the science corridor, we would check up on the goat baby. But, as time went on, things got busy and there were many new things to care about. The more boring school was, the more it made room for beauty. Biology classrooms became art studios. In English, I read sheet music. Liv and I wagged maths and did our maths homework in the music studios. In maths class, worksheets became templates for poetry. I liked to march down the corridor in full Elizabethan costume from the theatre wardrobe, clearing a path through the crowds, like a child holding a hand up to the ocean and commanding the waves to stop at her feet. Over time, we forgot about the goat.

Liv and I made our escapes. We ran to the beach to feel the sea sucking the wet sand from under our bare feet. Once, I climbed on the roof with Liv's help and ran from skylight to skylight along the corridor, waving to people below.

When school ended, Liv and I moved into a flat together for our first year of university. It was cold in our flat because heating costed money. Our other friends were never around unless we organised coffee a week in advance. I was bored, not knowing anyone in my classes, and having to write research reports about whether or not the response time to something flashing on a screen increased or decreased after something else flashed on a screen, the results of which had already been established by students in many other classes before. And there was no escaping anymore, because nobody cared to make me stay.

Our school counsellor once said that school is a microcosm of the universe, like a play in which you try out different roles before you have to pick one and perform, but it isn't really. School is just a bunch of rules. It either bores you to death, or, if you happen to be a particular kind of person, forces you to see things in a new way, to create. The more I hated university, the more I felt that, for me, high school, with its structure and stable social ecosystem, was my natural habitat.

'Wasn't high school kind of great?' I said to Liv one day in our flat. We were eating pasta and cheese, using our textbooks as trays, with a raw carrot on the side as punishment for the cheese.

'No,' said Liv. 'It was awful. It was boring, and everyone was bitching about everyone else, and we had to do NCEA so we hardly ever learned anything, and we weren't allowed to go to the bathroom without permission.'

I suddenly remembered the baby goat, in the cabinet all this time, with the gut-punched feeling of having remembered a pet left in a hot car. 'Do you remember the goat, Liv?'

'Oh yeah,' said Liv.

'He must have been there before we were born, and he'll be there after we're dead.'

'Well, we never asked how old he was.'

'Do you think we could steal him?'

We would have to buy a cabinet, we agreed, like the one in the science corridor. We could make our own science corridor. It would have a glass cabinet and room for new specimens as we collected them. A friend for our goat baby—a seahorse, maybe, or an unborn kitten. We would take them out from time to time to look at, and hold yearly funerals for them, like the ghosts at Hogwarts.

We planned our mission carefully. Liv would wear her old school uniform and a wig from the costume store, and she would go in just after school hours, posing as a student, and hide in a cupboard in our science classroom. Then, at midnight, dressed in black and sporting a balaclava, I would climb onto the roof and prise open a skylight. At midnight too, Liv would get out of her cupboard, take a hammer to the glass of the science cabinet, find the goat, and throw him back up to me through the open skylight. Then we would make our escape, her, walking casually out the back exit as if she had just stayed late studying, and me, clutching the goat like a cartoon diamond thief, running along the rooftop.

Iceland

The policeman led me down the stairs and out the main entrance of the supermarket. I tried to focus on the cool blue threads on his police vest, but all the same I could feel the gaze of the shoppers, I could feel them pinching the backs of their children's T-shirts, pushing their plastic shopping bags further back onto the fleshy parts of their arms. The rain had cleared, and the sky was cracking apart, the wind gasping through the sliding door as it opened, and the last water swelling from the guttering and bursting the puddles.

The policeman let me ride shotgun. On the radio, a class of twelve teenagers, trapped by floodwaters on a tramping trip, had been rescued by police helicopters and flown triumphantly to the hospital.

'So, are you gonna go back to your flatmates and have a laugh about this, then?' asked the police officer. It was such an obvious trick question that I couldn't see why he was asking it at all, unless he simply liked to think out loud.

'No,' I said.

'You haven't been caught before, have you?'

'No.'

'So, this isn't the first time you've stolen?'

'Uh...'

'You don't have to answer that,' he added quickly, and was quiet again.

At the police station I was locked in a cell. The walls were pale navy, the colour of hypothermia. On one side were steel bars. The two officers disappeared. Two minutes later, they returned, and I was moved to a smaller cell with a window into the next room where the officers filed my paperwork among shelves of boxes. There was a rectangular hole in the wall next to the window. As instructed, I took off my shoes and handed them, with my bag, through the hole.

The female officer took me to a third room with machines and pressed my palm into a scanning machine, rolling it from side to side, and then did each of my fingers and thumbs, holding them with two hands and pressing them firmly into the machine. Then I stood against the wall and she took a picture to post on the wall of shame in the staffrooms of the supermarkets. Wasn't it kind of a funny story, though? I thought to myself. All I had tried to steal was a can of tuna fish and a bottle of face wash.

A few weeks later, Marco, who worked in the chiller at one of the supermarkets, saw my picture on the wall of his workplace. 'How did I look?' I asked jokingly. But he paused. 'You looked scared,' he said.

They took me back to the cell and handed my belongings back through the hole in the wall, naming them one by one. 'Keys, scraps of paper, receipt, cellphone. Two dollars sixty in change. Pamphlets.'

They passed through the pamphlets I had made to advertise for flute pupils and the scraps of old labels I didn't want. I put everything back into my bag.

When the security guard had stopped me at the door and called me to his office above the supermarket, he had asked, 'Do you know why you're here?'

'I don't know,' I said. In a way, I didn't.

After my arrest, I tried to remember how the stealing had started. I recalled having been curious as to whether I would feel anything—guilt or anxiety. But I hadn't.

I don't remember the first thing I stole. It's not that I did it so often that this detail evades me; I was hardly a career shoplifter. But the thing itself wasn't important. I didn't steal beautiful or valuable things. I stole overpriced things. Things I kind of wanted but wouldn't pay for. Things that easily fitted in a pocket. Eventually, it was just a way to save money from time to time—buy most things and walk out with a few concealed.

I never stole from small or locally owned stores. Only from large department stores, chain stores and supermarkets. Large stores seem faceless. They are all scale, repetition and blank gleaming surfaces that no one can lay a personal claim to. There's no one person you're hurting. These stores allow for a certain amount of shoplifting in their budgets. The people I knew who shoplifted always brought up this fact as reassurance. You could argue that the companies pass that cost on to their innocent customers. But you could also argue that they don't have to—it's the company's choice, so who's robbing who? I thought of company men as giants, gliding up and down their glass elevators in anonymous suits. They could absorb little business costs like these if they wanted; it would mean nothing to them. They were overpaid anyway. On an American podcast called *Death, Sex and Money*, a shoplifter was asked whether she thought that shoplifting from large stores was a victimless crime. She said, 'I see it as a paper cut as opposed to stabbing someone.'

You can sit there reasoning with yourself for a long time, but it still never sits well. It's not easy to construct a new story about yourself that is strong enough to quell the other story, the one the policeman told with his silence.

Why do people shoplift? When I googled it, articles jumped out: 'When consumer behaviour goes bad . . .' 'Drug addiction . . .' 'Five reasons why . . .' Pictures of people wearing oversized sweatshirts. I closed the tab.

Five years passed before I finally made a real attempt to look up the research. It turns out there aren't many studies about motivations for shoplifting. I found a couple of American studies from the seventies. One of these papers, by a Harvard psychiatry professor named Donald Hayes Russell, claimed that stealing can stem from psychological unfulfillment. Most shoplifters are not in desperate need of food or clothing. They are, Russell said, destitute in other ways—emotionally, culturally; they're driven by a hunger for affection, for something to fill a gap in themselves. The cases he described from his 'Court Clinics' illustrate this. One 'poor little rich girl' said that stealing excited her sexually. A depressed housewife, 'envious of male power and freedom' but unable to express these thoughts, stole a two-dollar slip from a department store after arguing with her father. A manipulative young man who sounded almost sociopathic was caught stealing vegetables. A boy said to be 'schizoid'—a term covering symptoms which would now be categorised as Autism Spectrum Disorder—stole things such as chemistry sets and guns and kept them in his pockets, and 'gave the impression that they constituted a necessary part of himself', as if his body were a house and he was adding new rooms. He complained about his 'harsh, ungiving parents' and his siblings, who were always taking his things, with the implication that his stealing was a way of making a claim on the world or claiming himself back. A young girl whose parents gave her money to buy a dress for her school dance wandered instead into a thrift store and stole a cheap blouse, a 'shoddy thing, neither she nor her mother would think of wearing'. After months of talk therapy, it was discovered that she was 'beset with feelings of unfulfillment which stirred unconscious depths and led to the impulse to act out'. I wondered if I too had unconscious depths which might be stirred without my knowledge.

Russell did say, however, that the increasingly depersonalised nature of retail stores meant that many shoplifters didn't feel that they were robbing anyone. No guilt was felt. If this could be said in the 1970s, then the problem must be worse now, with self-check-out machines in supermarkets and pharmacies. In these cases, perhaps there is no deeper psychological explanation.

A few years later, in 1976, a social psychologist named

Robert Kraut surveyed college students in the US on shoplifting. His verdict was simple: 'Unlike drug addiction, alcoholism, insanity, or violent crime, shoplifting is not an exotic deviance with a complex motivation underlying it. The motivation is commonplace and indeed is the same as for normal shopping: the acquisition of goods at minimum cost.'

This study revealed a moral divide. Generally, those who had shoplifted said that they did it because they wanted something, didn't want to pay for it, and didn't think it likely they would be caught. They were also much more likely to claim that they approved of shoplifting. But those who had never shoplifted believed they would only ever shoplift under the condition of great necessity, or if they walked out with something by accident. Do shoplifters just have lower moral standards? Or is it more complicated?

Kraut mentioned something I remembered hearing from my social psychology professor a year or two after my arrest, but which I had not, at the time, connected to my own shoplifting: when our behaviour does not match our beliefs, it is easier to change our beliefs. My professor was an affable Irish bloke, prone to chatting about ideas like that in such a conversational way that, hearing it in the sleepy cadences of his lecture, the sun saturating the room the way it did at that particular time in the afternoon, I thought, well, didn't I always know that? And yet, it challenges everything that we tend to assume about causality and human behaviour. The fact that you yourself have shoplifted might be enough for you to approve of it, even if you hadn't had that opinion before you shoplifted. As I contemplated this, I felt my inner gears recalibrating, defending, reflexively, the concept of myself as a decent person. A bottle of face wash, every now and again, the occasional unauthorised discount. It really isn't a big deal though, is it?

From the random sample of students who participated in that study, 61 per cent had shoplifted at least once. In another study, one in twelve shoppers had recently stolen something. These studies were done in the US in the seventies and eighties—most of the research that looked for explanations seemed to be outdated—but a 2017 New Zealand survey showed that retailers lost just under 1.1 billion dollars to crime that year. That's more than a 92 per cent increase from what the same survey found in 2003. It's a fraction of the total profits, but still a lot of money and it's increasing with time.

In 1990, researchers tried to make sense of the sheer proportion of consumers who shoplift, saying:

> While this phenomenon is disturbing, we need not conclude that all or even most of these people are truly criminals. Nettler (1989, p. 37) observes that many people are contingently honest; they behave honestly most of the time but will occasionally slip into dishonesty if the circumstances are right. (Cox, et al. 1990)

When I read this, I wondered what it would take to be considered 'truly a criminal' if it is more than just someone who has committed a crime.

Criminal. I repeated the word in my head and felt uncomfortable. It would have been better if I'd stolen diamonds—something with class or value, or a canoe, as I had heard someone had done at an outdoor equipment store nearby. They'd simply picked up a canoe during business hours, nodded to the shop assistant as if it were all agreed, and walked out the door. If I had stolen a canoe, I would be a criminal of some value, with skill or bravery or a story. But I was a worthless criminal, a criminal of face wash and tuna.

After I walked home from the police station, I found my flatmates in one of their beds, playing a Pokémon computer game in a haze of weed smoke. I told them what had happened.

'Poor Maddy,' said Riley. 'I want to be supportive, but you are kind of spiralling away at the edges right now.' She giggled helplessly.

I imagined myself in her eyes—disintegrating, the way fire reaches out of itself into the space.

'Don't worry, Maddy,' said Liv. 'You'll get a diversion, for sure.'

'True, you're white and female. And a university student,' said Marco.

He had a point. My race and education made me more likely to receive a police diversion and get off lightly.

Months passed before the court date. A friend of mine from high school had a Disney-themed dress-up party and I decided to go as Captain Jack Sparrow. I hired a wig, made a hat out of black card, found a fake moustache, and dressed in pirate clothes.

When I arrived at my friend's house, she was wearing a minidress from Dotti.

'Where's your costume?' I asked her.

'It's here,' she said, showing me a miniature top hat. 'I'm the Mad Hatter. You know you're supposed to dress in minimal costume. Just wear nice clothes and add one thing, Maddy.'

'What's the point of that?' I asked.

Soon all of her other friends, who knew about minimal costume, turned up in minidresses and jeans with cute Minnie Mouse ears or rabbit ears, or red Snow White cheeks. I was secretly proud of myself. They sat in the lounge eating savouries with napkins. They practised goofy laughs, put on baby voices, and sang the theme song of their favourite anime series.

'Oh my God, we are so weird!' someone exclaimed happily.

I felt theatrically nostalgic as I perched on the edge of my friend's couch, watching them. We had been best friends once. 'We are going our separate ways,' I wrote lavishly in her card, 'what with you having acquired your fancy new office job— congrats!—and me having acquired a criminal record,' as if I were tumbling into some criminal underworld of secrets and thrills, like Jack Sparrow in a secret war with the institutions of government.

'What's that about a criminal record?' her mother asked me, having read the cards as they were laid out on the corner table.

'Oh, I was arrested, for shoplifting,' I said.

There was a silence. Everyone in the room looked at me and then looked away, confused or perhaps embarrassed for me. Of course, I hadn't actually acquired a criminal record. I was awaiting a court date, with the hope of getting a diversion which was, by definition, not getting a criminal record.

I couldn't tell my parents, and although my flatmates were some comfort, they had their own issues to deal with. I imagined prison life. I knew it wouldn't be like on TV, with the witty banter, drama and camaraderie. It would be sadder, and boring. But maybe, I thought wistfully, I would have time to develop decent abs, or a meditation practice.

When I arrived at the courthouse, security officers checked my bag for weapons. The waiting room was full. There was a man with tattooed forearms leaning his elbows on his knees. There was a young Samoan boy with two older women on either side, stony-faced in their best traditional dress. A weary-looking woman with two young children stared listlessly out the window. I tried to imagine what everyone's crime was. I looked at the tattooed man and thought, destruction of property? Assault? Maybe the tired woman had some kind of property dispute? I was probably wrong about all of it. What would they have thought I was here for, with my ginger almost-grown-out emo-fringe and my double-breasted scarlet coat? I hoped they would guess something anarchist, like egging a politician, which made me think that I had almost definitely judged my fellow criminals too harshly. Perhaps the guy with the tattoos was a highly skilled martial artist who had been in the wrong place at the wrong time, and the Samoan boy was a budding con artist like Matt Damon in *The Talented Mr. Ripley*, and the tired woman was running a telephone scam to feed the kids. I was just getting attached to my new cohort when my name was called and a well-dressed man beckoned me into a side-room.

'Good news,' he said. 'You've been offered a diversion.'

I wouldn't have a criminal record, but I would have 180 hours of community service.

*

120

I was assigned to wipe equipment down at the university gym. It wasn't so bad. I was invisible there, wiping invisible sweat off a hundred machines. When there were no more machines to wash, I washed the walls, the steps, the banisters.

I was wiping down a spin bike when I saw an old friend from high school on the elliptical behind me. She was a blond girl whom I had once pretended to eat for six hours in a muddy puddle for the feature film *I Survived a Zombie Holocaust*.

'What are you doing here?' she asked. I could have just said that I worked there, but instead I said, 'I'm doing community service, for shoplifting.'

'Oh,' she said, surprised, and then, slowly and without inflection, 'cool.'

For months I feared supermarkets. I had been trespassed from New World and Pak'nSave, and I even steered clear of the footpath around New World, unsure which bit of concrete was technically their property. I told my parents when I visited them that I just didn't like Pak'nSave, it was 'too yellow', so I wouldn't have to explain why I couldn't go in the store near their house.

Then, after a time, my fear was extinguished.

There was a girl who came to our flat often. Her name was Kelly. Kelly was blond and tall in a way that reminded me of a haystack. I remember her sitting on our living-room carpet and sorting half a kilogram of weed into little bags for resale. Apparently, her granny had died and left her a house.

'All my cousins hate me now,' she said. 'I mean, can't blame them. I do fuck-all and now I have a house. But it's their own fault, none of those cunts even bothered to visit her when she was alive. I'm the only one.'

It might have been that day, or another night, that she stayed over. She was on the run from the pigs, she said. She said her criminal record kept mysteriously being erased. She'd been arrested numerous times and they had to keep giving her diversions since she had no record. But she was 'laying low' at our flat that night.

'This cop saw me,' she said, 'a woman cop. She just looked right at me and I could see she knew who I was. I was just tripping so hard, I just fucking sketched out and ran, just got the fuck out of there, eh.'

The next afternoon Kelly and my flatmates were sitting out on the porch. I asked if someone could go to the supermarket and get me some ice cream.

'I'll pay you back,' I said.

'Why can't you go yourself?' said Marco.

'She's banned, dumbass,' said Liv.

'Oh, yeah.'

'Nah, don't worry about it,' said Kelly. 'For real, they banned me too, and I just go there anyway. They'll never notice you. They never notice me, and I look like a criminal.'

It was raining. I remember it was raining, because afterwards I tried to justify my actions. I didn't want to walk all the way into town. I just needed a few groceries, I wasn't going to steal anything, and time had passed. Surely nobody would notice me at the self-checkouts?

I was at the end of the canned food aisle when I saw the security guard watching me from behind the checkouts at the other end of the supermarket.

My heart began speeding, and I felt an awful knowledge in my gut as if something decomposing was stuck there. The security guard spoke to the girl at the counter and she looked at me too, beeping the items across without seeing them. I put down the groceries I was holding on the shelf in front of me. I started moving along the back aisle, but the security guard mirrored me, speed-walking between counters, popping up again at the end of each aisle, as if we were playing tag.

As I rounded the corner, I knew he had the advantage—the door was on his side of the supermarket—but, miraculously, as I sped through the self-checkout counters, he wasn't there. I glanced to the side and a crowd of young mothers with small children seemed to have blocked his way. And I was out the door. I was out and almost at the corner. I began to run. Surely his jurisdiction stopped there?

And then, somehow, with a dull, heavy swoop, he slid to a halt in front of me, blocking my path.

'Come on, now, game's up,' he said. 'You know where the office is.'

And I was gone. I saw my carefully cultivated identity flash before my eyes: Madison Hamill, Proxime Accessit of Queens, classically trained performance flautist, who once bungeed off the Auckland Harbour Bridge alone, who ran triumphantly along school roofs without even receiving a detention, who once performed, on aerial silks, a play she wrote involving a fake blood contraption and a fight to the death, which audiences had described as terrifying.

The thrill of fear was gone now. I was in the real eye of the hurricane; not the calm seat of power, but a space around which power formed a trap.

Nobody really knows why a hurricane has an eye. When air is spinning very fast, it causes updrafts that rise to the top of the storm and travel outwards to where it began, everything in perfect cycles as physics demands. Somehow, some air goes rogue and flows the other way, back into the centre and down again into the sea. Where the eye meets the sea, waves from all directions slam into each other and nothing on the surface of the water is safe.

My lawyer at the Community Law Centre wore shorts and sneakers in his office, a bare room with an old school desk facing the traffic.

'If we can show that having a criminal record would have consequences for your life that are disproportionate to the seriousness of the offence,' he said, 'we might have a chance of getting you a second diversion. Can you think of anything, particularly work or school plans, that would be disrupted? Travel plans, for instance.'

'Well,' I said, 'If I had a criminal record, they might not let me go to Iceland on exchange.'

'Have you made arrangements to go on exchange?' he asked.

'Well, I haven't applied yet, but I went to a seminar about it.' I liked the idea of Iceland, where everyone read books and was also a secret Viking. A place where the dark lasted for longer and the Northern Lights lit up the sky like an emergency finger painting and white foxes leaped in and out of snowy hollows. Where it was cold and distant and nobody knew anyone I knew, and I didn't speak the language. Iceland was even more appealing to me now. My life already felt like a long night on an icy tundra. I wanted my aloneness to be the kind you could take pictures of for social media.

'You'd need a letter from the decision-makers saying that a criminal record would stop you from going,' he said. 'The other thing that would help is if you were willing to do some counselling. It would show that you're taking responsibility.'

I went to the student exchange office first. It seemed unlikely that this would help. After all, if I hadn't had the financial support of my parents to consider an exchange trip to a foreign country in the first place, I wouldn't have had this opportunity to save myself from a criminal record, and that seemed like an unfair advantage that shouldn't be allowed. But it was my only chance.

A woman in an all-shades-fit-one foundation offered me a seat across from her desk. I tried to explain the situation. There was not much else going on in the room. The others in the office fell quiet as I spoke. All I needed was a note, I explained, that indicated that having a criminal record would stop me going on exchange.

'What was your crime?' she asked. There was a lack of warmth in her voice, which suggested suspicion.

'Where did you trespass?'

'What did you steal?'

'Well, that was silly, wasn't it?'

Something was missing, something I had always known in every conversation, even with strangers, something that was always there—empathy, that most fundamental middle ground. Now it wasn't there, and I found myself slipping, not knowing my lines.

'An email would be fine,' I said. 'It doesn't have to be

official.'

An older woman with an air of authority had sidled up beside me and was listening silently to the exchange.

'I'm afraid we make those decisions on a case by case basis after applications have been submitted,' said the first woman. 'With minor crimes, there's a chance it won't matter.'

'Even if you could say exactly what you just said, that there's a chance it might impact your decision, that might help,' I said.

'Well, we make those decisions on a case by case basis. It's not really up to me,' she said. 'You'd have to apply, but it would take a few months for a decision to be made.'

'Our concern,' the boss piped in, 'is that you're not really interested in going to Iceland and you're just using this to help your court case.'

'I really am interested,' I said. 'I was interested before all this. I went to a seminar.' But I could tell they didn't believe me.

I left the building so fast I couldn't breathe, shame burning in my spine.

I needed something else, some other proof. I wasn't sure I could live with this label for seven years, as if I were disguised in the middle layer of some wooden Russian nesting doll, with another, more convincing face obscuring my own. I had never been looked at like that before.

Criminal.

Criminal.

Why had I done it? If I was going to be a villain, I wanted to be a relatable villain. So I went searching for my backstory of psychological explanation.

The more I analysed and replayed my actions, trying to

126

make sense of them, the less sense I made. I recalled walking among the calm aisles, with the clean packaging in bright colours, everything separated and elevated by blank shelving, the bright, even light. What did I feel when I put the bottle of face wash in my pocket? That I needed face wash? It had the satisfaction that all new things had, the fullness of its contents like a ripe fruit, but it didn't matter that much to me. I didn't even look at prices, exactly, but felt the weight being lopped off the final price at the counter, a bargain.

That night, I stayed up late, googling.

Alexithymia: A personality construct characterised by the subclinical inability to identify and describe emotions in the self.

I knew that self-diagnosis was unreliable, and that it would be wrong to use some diagnosis as an excuse. I only wanted to understand. I tried on this label and it seemed to fit me, even more so when I found that it was often co-morbid with Autism Spectrum Disorder, which I had been diagnosed with as a young teenager.

The next day, a friend asked how I was.

'I don't know,' I shrugged.

'What's wrong?'

'Nothing, I just don't know how I am,' I said. I'd never really known.

'You can't not know,' he said. 'Just think harder.'

*

When I started high school, I knew that I had to be someone new. Not the girl who was shy, to whom people would say 'Cat got your tongue?' or 'Can you even talk?' or shout 'Loner' at. Not the girl who looked at the floor or followed the other kids around, trying to be invisible. I had watched these kids for so long, decoding them. I had figured out all the rules by then. But it was another matter to implement them.

The Rules

1. No pushing into a line, unless you were invited by someone to stand directly in front of them in the line, even though that still pushes everyone who is further down the line back by one place. Do not point out this logical discrepancy.

2. If anyone asks how you are, say, 'I'm good, how are you?' Don't answer the question. Don't pause to think about it.

3. People are listening not just to what you actually say but more to what you are saying with your body. If someone asks if you are okay, you must smile the appropriate amount when you say 'I'm fine', or else they will ask 'What's wrong?' This means your body language was incorrect, even though you really are fine. Insist you are 'just tired' to escape looking conspicuous.

4. Turn-taking in conversations is not A B A B A B. It's actually A B B A A B, with each person required to offer both an answer and a new question (they should be related in theme, but this is a secondary concern). But it can also be A B B A B A A B A B B, with minor variations. Turns are ceased when a story is being told.

5. What you say when it is your turn in a conversation is less important than the speed and tone with which you say it.

6. People only notice what is different. Therefore, if you mimic the behaviour of others effectively, you will be invisible to them. Counterintuitively, if you are too silent, stand alone, or fail to visibly direct your attention towards the speaker

dominating a group exchange, they will notice you.

7. Eye contact must not exceed three seconds and must occur at the beginning and end of each exchange.

8. Don't fold your arms too much.

9. Don't dawdle in unoccupied space. Always look like you are going somewhere. They can sense a loner.

10. You must always act as if people want to hear you speak.

11. You must love sports.

But it was hard to change my behaviour, because of rule 6: people only notice what is different. There is a period, after having first met a new person, during which a personality is established, and, within that period, personalities may be fluid without causing alarm. You can become whoever you want, and you will be solidified as such when the period of plasticity ends. I established this theory at a Girl Guides camp—since many of the bubbliest personalities were in a younger age group, I decided to pretend I was ten years old rather than twelve. I ran around playing tag with the younger girls, chattering, playing Truth or Dare and laughing at rude words in sign language. Though I was exhausted at the end of that weekend, for the first time since I was very small, I had been a bubbly person—the highest class of person. I knew that in order to be a bubbly person permanently, I needed a completely new environment. High school came at the right time. The moment I arrived I began to implement my new persona.

Me: 'Hello, I'm Maddy.' (Implied question: what's your name?)

Sarah: 'I'm Sarah. What do you think of Queens so far?'

Me: 'It's all right. My sister goes here, she's in Year 11. You have really long hair.' (Delay question, as the statement requires a response.)

Sarah: 'Thanks.'

Me (continuing with question): 'What primary school did you go to?'

Sarah: 'Port Chalmers, it's really small there, I don't know anyone here. What about you?'

Me: 'Green Island. Rachel went there too, and Jessica— both the Jessicas actually . . .'

I was away! I implemented the rules so well that I became a chatterbox. I was exhausted for the first few weeks, but I established my place in the mid-periphery of a group slightly to the left of the cool group. Habits became cemented, and I became comfortable in my new role over the years to come.

The only problem was that my newfound confidence didn't extend to social circumstances outside my high-school friend group. When I joined an orchestra, I found that the people there had already established their friend groups. Established groups were insurmountable obstacles to me. Maybe it was partly because at orchestra practice everyone interacted primarily through the tradition of mingling over a table of pizza or sushi and cups of tea. It was loud and there were people on all sides. I tried to look occupied, walking to the food and back to my position against the wall, looking into my tea, going to the bathroom and returning, staring at my phone while frowning as though interpreting a text message. I longed for the break to end so we could return to the music, where my turn was marked on the page and my mind could be entirely occupied, leaving no space for anxiety, no space for thought.

After my first year of high school, a family friend named Karen came to stay with us over the summer. She was doing a PhD in autism spectrum disorder, a long-term research project that involved interviewing and diagnosing hundreds of kids. She had lived with us for a year back when I was eleven, so we thought of her as an extension of our family.

Karen had severe depression. Sometimes she would stop moving or speaking and lie on the floor as if something were weighing her down. It made me feel powerless to watch her struggle like this. But Karen was strange in another way. When she was well, she sometimes didn't know when to stop talking. She would chatter excitedly about psychology or music, or she would argue theology with my dad. She avoided eye contact and was scared of milk and vacuum cleaners and telephones, and these behaviours were not the things that made her depressed. They were part of her, because they were signs of Asperger's syndrome (then a category on the autism spectrum). I gathered that Asperger's was something that very smart people had; it meant their brains were different in ways that were inconvenient to bothersome 'neurotypicals'. You could get access to private rooms in the university if you had Asperger's, where everyone had to be quiet. There was a swipe card to open the doors, just like tapping bricks to get into Diagon Alley.

At the end of my first year of high school, my reports all read, 'Maddy is very intelligent but does not participate in class discussions.' I was told that my teachers didn't know what to do with me.

One day, Karen was preparing for a conference about autism spectrum disorder. 'Maddy can come along and be my example,' she joked to my parents.

'Why would you say that?' my mum said. 'Why would you suggest that she's autistic? That's not okay. She's right here. She can hear you.'

'I don't care,' I said. I really didn't.

A few days later, after my parents had adjusted to the idea and talked it through with Karen and each other, Karen asked if I wanted to be tested.

'Okay,' I said. I'd always loved tests. So Karen tested me with the tools she used in her research, observing how I interacted with various toys and art tools. I was asked to read a story and was tested on my vocabulary and planning skills. Afterwards, she scored my test and spoke to my parents.

When they called me over, my mother, who could never control her expressions, had a look on her face as if she were telling me I had terminal cancer. 'Maddy,' she said, 'Karen thinks that you have Asperger's syndrome.'

It annoyed me, the way she looked at me. What Karen had 'discovered' changed nothing. If I were abnormal in some way, then I always had been and always would be, so what was the point of suddenly being sad about it? What exactly was she mourning?

'Okay,' I said.

Karen gave me the official report afterwards. It was titled 'Assessment report: Confidential'. I had never seen myself described in such detail.

Madison's use of sentences was always correct but some of her speech was more formal than most individuals with the same level of complexity, but was not obviously odd. Her speech tended to be rather flat though at times exaggerated in tone. At times, Madison started to speak in an accent or used inappropriately rapid speech. Madison rarely spontaneously offered or asked for information. Her conversation had little reciprocity ... In general, Madison did not make consistent eye contact throughout the assessment to regulate her social interactions, though she did make some facial expression to the examiner. She showed pleasure in her own actions but did not communicate this to the examiner using integrated eye contact, facial expression and language ... Most of her communication was either object-orientated, or responses to questions with little social chit-chat.

The document described my behaviour and the results of each test, and at the end, the diagnosis. It said I had received a score of 27.

90% of people on the autism spectrum receive a score of 30+. This assessment is written more towards males with ASD and ASD seems to present differently in females. Only 12% of females score more than 22 on this assessment. Based on these assessments it appears Madison's current presentation is consistent with Asperger's syndrome or High Functioning Autism.

The more comfortable I became in my new bubbly personality at school, the more dubious my diagnosis began to feel to me. I was capable. There was another girl in our school who was really autistic, and she spoke in a monotone. I wasn't at all like her. None of my friends thought I had Asperger's when I explained my diagnosis to them. I wasn't Rain Man, or Sheldon Cooper from *The Big Bang Theory*. And yet, I still wondered if there was secret language going on around me. I thought of the characters in novels who could look at someone and say he had a spark in his eye, or she looked into his eye and electricity tingled up her spine, or he had expressive eyes, or beady eyes or cold eyes, or 'there was a shift in the atmosphere of the room', with everyone coming to a mutual understanding that I could not feel. Maybe I was just shy. I didn't feel shy—I thought that shyness implied cowardice, but maybe I was. Everyone was always saying so. I tried to expose myself to the things I feared—loud music, dancing, crowds, and worst of all, 'mingling'.

I volunteered to travel on a sailing ship for ten days. The first few days were okay. I slept in a room with twenty girls, I ran around the ship from dawn till 10pm, being constantly sociable. I chatted, I learned everyone's names, I survived. But I began to lose energy after day three, and somehow, while others deepened their connections with one another, my connections remained distant. I was so exhausted that on the last day, the day we forty teens sailed the ship by ourselves all the way back to Auckland Harbour, though I wanted to participate, I faked sickness and stayed in bed till midday.

In the years that followed, I returned to the ship as a volunteer crew member four times. It was always the same. No matter how much I forced myself to face my fears, I could not change. I began to return to the diagnosis, and to research the subject. I read almost every book in the public library on the subject, which was two little shelves about a foot in width. I read everything I could, trying to figure out such a simple thing. Was I 'on the spectrum', or not?

The core texts on autism seemed to suggest that I wasn't. People with autism, they said, were predominantly male, overtly logical, and liked lining things up in order. They all seemed to be obsessed with trains. But there were also women who had ASD. Some of them were not straight lines and trainsets kinds of girls—they were imaginative, in a world of their own and struggling to form close connections, but they were coping, learning to mimic the behaviours of their peers.

I came across articles by the researcher Tony Attwood, who believed that the reason so few women were being diagnosed with Asperger's was not that it was less prevalent in women, but because female expressions of Asperger's were less obvious and were less likely to cause concern to others. Many women with Asperger's just learned to adapt. Attwood believed that because of the way girls are socialised, they're more motivated to learn social skills. I learned that the first understandings of Asperger's were derived from studies using exclusively male subjects. While the dominant assumption was that ASD was a kind of extreme version of the male personality—logic, precision, order, lack of engagement—most of the people on the spectrum who were writing about it seemed to be female, and they were questioning this.

I read one book that collected the memoirs of a diverse range of women who had ASD. I saw little snatches of myself in all of them. But many were much worse off than me. I thought: I get along okay, I'm a high achiever, so who am I to claim this label? Once again, clarity was out of reach. I tried to accept the task of being different in a way that couldn't be understood, floating around in the murky edges of what could be categorised.

By the time I finished high school and was choosing a university major, I had spent so long observing the behaviour that most people didn't question, that I decided to study psychology.

I was excited when my professor spoke about autism briefly. But afterwards, I wished he had said more or not spoken at all. He said that one of the defining features of the autism spectrum was a deficit in imagination. Then he moved on to other subjects. I felt powerless. How then, I wanted to ask, do all those women in that book make sense? How do I make sense?

*

I went to a counsellor, as my lawyer had suggested. I said I had googled this trait of alexithymia, which was related to ASD, and that while it wasn't an excuse, it might have influenced my mental state and decision-making abilities at the time. He didn't say this was a ridiculous theory, or a weakly disguised excuse in the genre of psychological lingo; he just nodded and said variations of 'How do you feel about that?'

I asked to see a psychologist so that I could be officially tested for ASD. I couldn't tell if I was going to the psychologist because a diagnosis might help my legal case, however tenuous the connection might be, or if the case was an excuse to ask for a diagnosis when I hadn't felt legitimate in my claim to seek one before. All I knew was that I craved categorisation—a brand new label, with a story attached. I wanted a reason for shoplifting, but I wanted a reason for everything, as if I were a puzzle that could only be solved by storytelling. Why did I so often feel like I was stealing the attention and time of other people by being around them? Why did I feel so far underwater when everyone with their ordinary feelings and chit-chat were floating above me? I wanted a reason for not having a reason and I would steal one if I could.

The psychologist asked me what made me think I had ASD. I explained that I found eye contact difficult, that I felt overwhelmed in crowds, that loud noises were painful, that conversations had always been difficult, and that though I was much improved since I was thirteen, I sometimes hid in corridors to avoid mingling at social events.

'And do you think that you are impaired in your home or school life?'

I paused, then tried to explain. 'Well, I feel overwhelmed in large spaces like lecture halls and the library and find it difficult to make friends.'

'Those are symptoms,' she said. 'What I need to know is whether these symptoms mean you are impaired in your home or school life.'

I recognised her wording, of course. She was reciting the defining criteria for ASD given in the official Diagnostic Statistical Manual. It was a simple enough question, and maybe if I'd just said yes she would have referred me for testing, but I thought of how I had gone to high school deciding to be a new person, how I had observed and learned how to put my brain away and chatter mindlessly, how the timing and tone of voice mattered more than content, how to look at someone's eyebrows as if through a magic eye book, so that it looked like you were making eye contact, and just how long that was necessary. How I had walked my fear into crowded rooms, had dared myself a million times, had danced mimicking the movements, pretending not to be threaded with anxiety. And I was a success, a bubbly person, in certain scenarios, even, an A-grade student, a winner of local poetry awards. To claim 'impairment' would be to deny all of that.

I said, 'No.' And that was that. I was sure now that I was going to be labelled a criminal and never go to Iceland or anywhere else. As I waited for the court date I tried to curl up in a ball. I avoided mirrors and open spaces. I churned out papers on social psychology and disappeared into my room to binge-watch my thoughts away. I tried to think of myself less as a linear cause-and-effect puzzle and more as a handbag holding a collection of organs and curiosities—a heart, two lungs, a long spool of fear, a tangle of experiences and a bottle of something brand new and imperishable that I had taken from the world and couldn't give back.

When I arrived at the court I was ushered into another side room. My lawyer was there, in a real suit this time, his black shoes shining like new cars. 'Good news,' he said. 'You're being given a second diversion.' And he gave me another date to be at the police station.

The next wait was just as long, but not as heavy. Something felt unclenched inside me.

'Remember,' said Marco, 'tell them your parents know. Otherwise they'll call them up. Just act scared and apologetic.'

'You'll be fine,' said Liv. 'Just accept whatever they tell you. It's okay, don't worry. If I hug you will you run away?' I rolled my eyes and accepted the hug.

At the police station, I followed the officer into the lift, and along a maze of hallways, into a small room. An officer was sitting behind a large wooden desk.

'Take a seat,' she said.

'Would you be willing to meet with some people from Restorative Justice?' she asked after we had been through the formalities. I said yes, though I wondered briefly what would have happened to me if I had said no.

The restorative justice people visited me in my flat to prepare me for the meeting. They were two blond women in white sneakers, like my lawyer had been at our first meeting. I had tried to tidy up the main area of the flat in preparation, but the kitchen proved too big a task. It was hard enough to remind my flatmates to clear off for the afternoon.

'We're not here to judge,' said the older of the two, as they sat down across from me together on our one couch, where I hoped they couldn't see the kitchen. 'We're just here to help you know what to expect.'

'Okay,' I said. 'How does it work? Do I meet with someone from the supermarket?'

'Well, the thing is,' said the woman, 'the supermarket doesn't have the time or staff to send a representative, so they will be represented by one of our lovely volunteers, who is a local businesswoman. Think of it as a chance for both of you to explain your point of view. Our volunteers have lots of experience in local businesses, so they represent not just the supermarket but the wider community as well. And they'll listen to your perspective, so it's a chance to make amends with the community.'

'Okay,' I said. 'What should I do to prepare?'

'If I were you, I would write a letter of apology to the super-market, and also take a chance to look on the supermarket's website to find a charity that they support and consider giving a donation. This will show that you care, and that you want to give back to the community.' I hadn't realised I was stealing from 'the community' until then, so I took a moment to absorb this. *The community.* Was it really like that, I wondered, like a club with secret handshakes and you could pay your way in if you failed the initiation ritual? That night I dreamed I was in a very crowded room where everyone was mingling, and I was pretending to do the same. Someone noticed that I wasn't offering anything of value to the others in the room but was just hiding in their company so as not to look alone, and they turned around and demanded I tell a joke as payment for my continued presence. I told them it seemed a fair enough request, but I couldn't think of a joke, so I had to leave.

The following Tuesday I turned up at a small community room, nervous but relieved. After this, I could move on, pretend that none of it had ever happened. The two restorative justice people were there, and a woman named Jill. Jill was representing the wider community.

'I'm a small-business owner,' she said. 'It makes me very upset that people like you choose to break the rules like this. I don't think you understand that your actions have consequences.' Her voice was shrill. 'You cost us time and money, and the upshot is, there's no trust left in our communities. As soon as one or two people like you decide to take advantage, the suspicion remains. People like you are the bane of our existence. And big supermarkets like the one you stole from have to hire more than one security guard, and that's money spent on paying each security guard's salary, taking money out of business profits, all because people like you think you can break the rules.'

I thought for a moment that I was quite glad that the security guard had a job, because he seemed like a nice man who felt valued for his work. But I told Jill that I was very sorry and deeply ashamed, and that I had already written a letter of apology and made a contribution to a charity that the supermarket supported. Jill asked me about my future and I said that I was a university student, with plans to visit Iceland. Much was made of this, as if my potential might outweigh my crimes after all.

'Hold on to what's right,' Jill said to me, 'and you'll be a fine person.'

The Participant

Once, I decided to be a doctor. I liked the idea of looking at someone and understanding what was wrong with them, and of collecting clues and having epiphanies like on the TV show *House M.D.* I believed in this decision for weeks, dreaming of wearing white lab coats and marching through wards saying 'Start her on this drug' and 'Get me a scalpel' and 'Chop that limb off or he'll bleed to death'.

I believed it until I could no longer suppress my underlying knowledge that doctorhood was quite different from what it was on television, with many more people dying slowly of common diseases than dramatically of uncommon ones, and that it was much more a matter of filing paperwork, explaining the inevitable and the best or worst case scenarios, and smiling sympathetically at the snotty-nosed and fatigued, asking them personal questions, looking them in the eye as they answered and telling them the things they needed to hear: that there was a name for their particular kind of snotty nose or fatigue, that they weren't alone. None of this would have been so bad for a people person. I was not a people person. Surely only people people would be capable of such an advanced level of human interaction?

I decided to join the army, for the routine. This decision seemed perfect for two weeks, until I could no longer ignore the problem of having to shoot people.

My mother said I should be a librarian. And how dare she think that! A mousy librarian. It was like early retirement for shy people. I did not like being put in a box, and resolved to create an opposing identity in order to avoid such categorisation: I would study psychology.

As a psychologist I would be hired to be an expert on other people's minds, and I would 'swan around' in businesswear in high-rise buildings. 'Swan around' was a phrase that I assumed from my mother's usage meant 'to move in a privileged and leisurely manner'. I would point to charts and say, 'No, don't you see that's not how people will behave in reaction to this or that business prospect or political situation.' I would have a corner office overlooking somewhere far away, perhaps Washington, DC, where I would advise the CIA on negotiations with kidnappers. As an expert on people, I would also, by now, have become a people person.

Shortly after I made my new career plan, I came across a play with a character named Pam, whom I 'diagnosed' with schizophrenia. An opportunity to study Pam further came in the form of a Drama assessment: 'Write and perform, in groups, a five-minute extension of an existing play'. I researched what it was like to be schizophrenic. I watched documentaries and read symptom descriptions and first-person essays. The best way to convey the experience of schizophrenia to an audience was soon clear to me: I would choreograph an aerial silks routine. It seemed only right that Pam's auditory hallucinations should be represented by a figure dangling above her, heavy and spider-like. My friend played the part of Pam and I myself played the part of Pam's hallucination in the aerial silks. As I dangled overhead I called out words like *bitch*, *cunt*, *stupid freak*, the worst things I could think of—until Pam fought back and stabbed me in the chest with the beak of a large bird, which I had found on a family holiday and boiled in bleach to serve as an added layer of death symbolism. And then I—the hallucination—appeared to die, but so did Pam, looking down shocked at her own chest to find that she had in fact stabbed herself.

Being a psychologist must be just like this, I thought. Being able to hang out with real people like Pam and to visualise what was happening in their minds.

The auditorium for my first psychology lecture was full of students. Unfortunately, it turned out that before you could learn about hallucinations you had to learn about eyes. The professor explained how the eye translated the world—its layers of cells firing or not firing, first in response to light or dark, with each little rod in the forest that was the back wall of the eye latching on to its own little speck of the outside world, like a reverse map. The signals passed through the optic nerve and into a chamber in the brain where the groups of firing-in-response-to-light-or-dark-specks led to other cells firing in response to columns of light or dark in particular orientations. And those signals of firing or not-firing were passed on to two places at once, so that, on the one hand, the shapes signalled by the patterns of firing triggered cells that responded only to the specific concept of 'hand', or 'laptop', or 'professor', or 'whiteboard', and on the other, different cells detected the movement of the professor's hands as she gesticulated at the whiteboard. It was possible to have a tumour in the movement-detection department and still see perfectly well otherwise, so that the world appeared like a series of photographs—the glass would be almost empty and then it would be overflowing, and you couldn't see how it got to be that way. The firing went on all over the brain; you could listen in using gelled electrodes plastered to your skull, and it was like listening to an ants' nest. And all of that noise was, somehow, an explanation for my ability to see the professor frown at the end of her pointing stick as it wavered in midair, and to recognise from her expression that she had forgotten something.

I began to feel numb wandering the bright, airy corridors, slipping quietly into lecture theatres and then out again with my head down, waiting patiently for one of the lecturers to confess they'd cracked the secret to telepathy and were going to teach us, finally, to understand one another. The lecture slides were full of results and theories, many of which I had always assumed to be true anyway, like the idea that difficult tasks are performed better when you feel a certain level of anxiety. Too little and you're unmotivated; too much and you're incapacitated by it. Or the idea that we don't understand ourselves through introspection—turning inwards to examine our character, as if it were some kind of skeleton to our X-ray vision—but through the same way we understand other people, by observing patterns in their behaviour, by making inferences and interpretations.

Several times a year, psychology students could sign up to participate in a study for extra credit. You'd be led down a narrow corridor to a small office space with a computer, and the researcher would leave the room so as not to influence your decisions. Maybe the researcher would say, 'Take all the time you need,' but then she would be somewhere close by, no doubt comparing the time you took with the time previous participants had taken. I was always slow at these sorts of questions. They usually required you to pick a number between one and five to describe the amount or degree of something that didn't seem like it could be categorised in amounts or degrees. 'On a scale of one to five, how much do you agree with the statement "I am an anxious person"?' 'To what extent would you agree with the statement "I have just as much to offer as the next person"?' 'To what extent would you agree with the statement "I make decisions based on the information at hand"?'

In one study, teenagers participated in ten-day voyages on a ship with no internet where they were taught to sail. There were forty teens on each voyage, and for three of these trips, the teens were surveyed before, after and five weeks following the trip. Through this experience, the surveys showed, these teenage trainees became increasingly 'resilient'; able to deal with challenges in adaptive and productive ways, compared with a control group, and these changes were long term. The teens' newfound resilience was driven by their feelings of acceptance into the group onboard the ship. It wasn't just about group cohesion, but the conquering of adversity. The worse the weather was, for example, the stronger the bonds that were formed and the more resilient the trainees became. Perhaps seeing each other jump into the shivering sea the same way or climb the masts hand over hand until the ship looked as small as their own body made them feel as though their fear was shared.

I'd been on the ship when I was a teen. The ship had tacked and gybed around the Bay of Islands, and I'd watched the others, one by one, succeed at the ritual of bonding. Most of them had seemed nervous when they stepped on board, but once on the ship the world back on land seemed to disappear until it was just a concept. They grew new, tough sea skins over their old ones, and I watched a fierce love growing between them. The sea, a self-sustaining engine, rocked them into a dream. Some of the trainees found it harder than others to do the compulsory jump each morning into the sea when it was still dark, the sea–sky a dull green like a bruise. There was one trainee, her legs like milk, her bony chest pressed into the red buoyancy aid, who looked into the green–black shiver of the water as if it could rise up to eat her. Every morning she shook before jumping, then screamed as she jumped. But every day, she jumped.

When everyone else was solidifying their group bonds, something was pulling me away. Around day five, I sat in the mess hall and watched the animal transformation that was taking place, the voices gaining volume like a hive about to swarm. I felt exhaustion overcome me. The energy required to break into the rhythms of the mass conversation was too much. I smiled at the right times to look as if I were still there, but in my mind I had already gone home. Next time, I thought, I would be better. I would laugh more, memorise a joke to tell, open myself to experience.

Returning home after the ship was like returning from a different country, as if the ship and the rest of the world were two dreams rubbing alongside each other, and nothing could be clearly remembered in one when you were in the other. I wondered why the psychology I learned was never enough to explain why I seemed to be an exception to the inexplicable effects of the ship, why simply being around so many people made me power down rather than open up.

Every year or so after that, I returned to the sailing ship as a crew member. I thought I would get better if I just kept practising. I knew that avoidance wasn't a sustainable coping mechanism and that anxiety could be made 'extinct' by repeated exposure. But each time I returned, I felt overwhelmed and withdrew into myself.

The time I went to orchestra camp, I hid in my tent and waited till the last minute to make my way to the auditorium for practice. The tent's walls were close and red like the sun through an eyelid. Where the outer and inner layers of it touched, they clung and shimmered. It was very hot and the tent leaned in towards me. I could hear people laughing as they passed on their way to the auditorium. I waited, staying very still, until everything was quiet except the wind in the fabric, before climbing out.

I ran until I was in the shadow of the bunkroom buildings, glancing behind me, and then began walking at an even, brisk pace towards the auditorium, as if I had nothing in my head but 'What a lovely day it is' and 'Was that a tūī? I think it was a tūī'.

In biopsychology I learned the difference between fear and anxiety, which it turned out everybody was still confused about. *The Diagnostic and Statistical Manual of Mental Disorders* said that fear was about 'real' or imminent threat, while anxiety was the anticipation of a future threat, but that they 'overlapped', presumably when it came to real imminent future threats. My professor had a new theory that fear and anxiety could be defined by the behaviour they produced. First, you put a rat in a cage that looked just like its natural environment. Then you made a cat walk past and observed the rat's behaviour. Then you gave that behaviour a name. Fear could be defined by avoidance behaviours (freeze or flight), whereas anxiety could be defined by a tentative approach to the danger zone, such as the rat's return to foraging after the cat was believed to have moved on. The rat's particular response depended on its perceived distance from danger.

Fear and anxiety occur in different parts of the brain, too. Social anxiety is mostly a product of the dorsolateral prefrontal cortex, a region associated with planning. A socially anxious person is constantly turning towards and backing away from the danger zone; she is in a constant negotiation of approach and avoidance, where the approach is ultimately the only right choice, because the thing she wants is also the source of anxiety. Compare this with obsessive compulsive disorder. OCD is an avoidance-based disorder—what my professor would think of as a fear disorder. It consists of another sort of negotiation: if I carry out this action—if I knock thirty times or flick this switch off and on again—bad things will not happen. OCD is mostly associated with the ventral prefrontal stream, where external stimuli and emotion interact.

The closer the danger is perceived to be, the deeper and older the brain structures that are involved become. When the perceived distance from the danger is zero, fear and anxiety come from the same place, and are called panic, and this occurs somewhere primal, close to the brain stem. In a state of panic, a rat will fight a cat.

There are some things about all this that still confuse me. If someone believes a shark is in the water, for instance, and they still jump, in that moment are they afraid or are they anxious? Is it their behaviour which defines the mental state that was their obstacle? Is it fear when you are hiding in your tent, and anxiety when you leave the tent? Other situations don't offer an easy way of approaching the threat or running from it. These situations have nothing to do with death, and much more to do with the gap you can feel between the person you are and the person you wish to be. Sometimes, I think I feel anxiety about things that have already happened. Can you be anxious about the past?

Fear has a reputation for being stronger and more legit-imate than anxiety. You should fear your enemies, for instance. You wouldn't say, 'He struck anxiety into the hearts of his enemies.' I can't help thinking anxiety is really the more noble of the two. If you are afraid, you run away or play dead or stab your enemy through the heart to make the danger go away. But if you are anxious, it's because you have chosen to move in with your enemy and take up the housework of living in the danger zone.

*

Every Tuesday evening I waited in the shadow of the university building for a black vehicle to arrive. Inside were two or three other people in leggings. The car was driven by a man who had a missing thumb and metal joints. 'There's more metal in me than not,' he once said. 'Every time I have a new injury, they ask me how much pain I'm in, on a scale from one to ten. I say, oh, a three, and my doctor says, she knows me, so she'll interpret that as a seven.' He laughed. 'I was for real though, I've had my spine done in, an arm injury's not gonna bother me. I was back on my bike the next day.' The metal man had raced motorcycles and cars around the world, and he could fly a plane. I got the sense that his bravado wasn't a shield for any secret fears, but an honest reflection.

How could pain or fear, or shame, belong on a rating scale when the only comparisons we can make are with our own experiences, when a three for one person is a seven for another in the same circumstances?

The metal man put on Lana Del Rey and her sleepy metallic voice carried the car through the cold lights of the city. We arrived at a primary school across town where we all got out and waited in the dark playground for the doors of the school hall to open and the small children learning karate to bow and file out the door. Then the hall was ours, and we stretched, and then carried the mats from the corner so that one mat was below every aerial silk. Each of us had our own island and we could disappear up to the ceiling like children climbing trees. We climbed up fast and then cocooned ourselves just below the ceiling beam, wrapping ourselves in the silk so only one leg dangled out of the fabric bulb, and there we could finally think.

Across the hall, dancers emerged out of their own cocoons to dangle or spin. One woman left her crutches on the ground and pulled herself up, toes pointed, spinning and folding herself into the splits. Another girl whose immune system was eroding her joints was now able to lift up her whole body with one arm. A girl named Silkie rolled herself up, as if gravity had reversed, and twisted outward to hold on by her feet. It was like the silk had bloomed and she was the pistil at its centre. The metal man copied her with stiff movements. I used to think, when I watched him, that my movement detection had suddenly ceased to work.

'We're all freaks here,' the metal man said proudly.

We gathered around from time to time to watch someone perform a trick, or laugh when someone managed to tangle themselves up in a particularly ridiculous manner halfway to the ceiling. But mostly, my island was my own in which to embroider myself into any new contortion I could imagine.

I've been learning about comparative psychology, the study of the behaviour and mental processes of non-human animals so that comparisons can be made between species. From what I've been learning so far, there is one group of comparative psychologists who spend a lot of time training chimpanzees to do things that humans can do, like use language and solve problems. This is mostly because the researchers really like having pet chimps and impressing their friends but also making a point about human evolution and how we're not so different from animals. Other comparative psychologists focus on pigeons. They train their pigeons to do similar things to the chimpanzees in order to prove how unimpressive the chimps are. If a pigeon can do it, it can't have been a real human-like ability after all, and this therefore reasserts the superiority of humans. It takes longer for the pigeons to learn, for sure, but they always get there. For instance, one psychologist insisted that his chimpanzees could carry out a real conversation, but another psychologist convinced his postgrad students to spend three years teaching his pigeons to converse using coloured buttons with symbols on them, so he was able to use the research as fodder for a scathing review. One researcher even taught their pigeons to tell a Monet from a Picasso. The pigeons were on a strict reward regimen for many weeks and months, with postgrad students carrying out the mind-numbing process of giving food and denying food, giving and denying. If the reward was right, this research seemed to show, even something with a brain made for distinguishing grain from dirt could be taught to perform in a way that appeared unnatural.

I lay on my mattress one evening beneath the aerial silk that twisted all the way up to the ceiling beam. The sounds of rustling and twirling fabric were all around me, and the hard thump of bodies landing. I was restless. I felt an urge to run through a trick or two.

I climbed until I was level with the pigeons, which hum just outside the upper windows—*coo, coo*, their bodies vibrating against the rafters. I tied myself in a complicated knot and dropped, not fast the way I did years ago in the play with Pam, but slowly, my torso tensing as the fabric tightened its grip. I spun around and around till I was a metre off the floor. As I looked down I thought I could see a version of myself still huddled on the mattress below. That version—or part—of myself seemed at peace. It had shut me out. It had its eyes closed and was enjoying the comfort of my mattress. I didn't speak to it, even though I wanted to yell that familiar set of insults to remind it that it was failing to perform the way it should. I took a deep breath and looked at the other part of myself, and for once, felt kindness. I sang, 'Coo, coooo,' in a soothing manner, and although it took all my strength, I untwisted my legs, flipped over, and pulled myself up again until I reached the ceiling.

I Will Never Hit on You

1

Some friends and I were speeding along a dirt road in Namibia when a one-horned oryx darted across the road. Dust flew backwards from his hooves so that it seemed the world was moving out of his way.

'One of its horns has been hacked off,' I said.

My friend saw it differently. 'It's a unicorn!'

But a one-horned, horse-like oryx is not a unicorn, just as a unicorn whose horn is hacked off by poachers does not become a horse. It makes a difference whether something has been lost or was simply never there to begin with.

If you take the poacher's machete and use it to chop off his testicles, that's problematic. If, however, an inhibiting factor was never produced in the womb of the poacher's mother to begin the development of male sex characteristics in the foetus, there wouldn't be any testicles, and the poacher would not be missing anything. They'd be a female poacher.

But this essay isn't about that.

2

My mother used to say I was mysterious. She wrote me an acrostic poem for my twenty-second birthday and the first letter was 'M', and she wrote 'mysterious'. Not majestic, mesmerising or maverick. Mysterious. And what she really meant was that I keep secrets. I'm uncommunicative. In those twenty-two years, I hadn't fully let her know me.

3

There was a word I searched for. I wanted to know that the people whom the word represented were alive and doing things that weren't just explaining what the word meant or talking about the word with one another. Afterwards, I thought about deleting my search history in order to delete the word from my search history.

The Spinoff: What I Learned From my First Month of Drafting Tinder Bios for Cash. 2018. ('A staggering range of people have approached me—old, young, bisexual, █████, techies, musicians . . .')

The New Zealand Herald: Janelle Monae Inspires Spike in Searches for 'Pansexual'. 2018.

Al Jazeera: Inside the World of China's Ultra-Rich. 2016. (Asians on TV are 'stuck in stereotyped roles—█████ Asian males and hypersexualised Asian females.')

ABC News: The Desirable Lesbian Crip. 2015. ('Sex and

disability isn't something that most people have thought a lot about. Or, if they have, it's often in stereotypical ways: disability as a tragedy, people with disabilities as powerless, weak, dependent, ██████, passive or (in the case of intellectual disabilities) as hyper-sexual, uncontrollable.')

Associated Press: no results

CNN: Gang Raped and Left Without a Choice: Living with Disability in India. 2018. ('"She is considered ██████, unattractive or on the other extreme: desperate and only wanting sex," said Goyal.')

New Yorker: A Year Without Oliver Sacks. 2016. ('Certain dandelion species only reproduce ██████.')

Otago Daily Times: Brooke Shields Remembers '██████' [Michael] Jackson. 2009. ('Shields said that as Jackson grew up, "the more ██████ he became to me."')

New York Times: The Revolution Has Been Televised. 2018. Tina Fey's character Liz Lemon is 'frumpy and absolutely fine with that ██████.'

Stuff.co.nz: ██████: Can a Relationship Without Sex Work? 2017. ('Canadian academic Anthony Bogaert has written the first major book on this subject, *Understanding ██████*.')

4

'And so, I stabbed him in the eye with a pencil,' Rachel sighed, smiling knowingly. 'I had such a crush on him. Were you there, Maddy?'

'No, I don't remember it,' I said. 'I only remember you telling me about it.'

We were thirteen or fourteen, in our pyjamas, having

showered and doused the bunkrooms of our school camp with a vaguely floral blend of cheap spray perfumes that came in smells like 'pink' and 'summer crush'.

Rachel gave her wet handful of ringlets one last tug with the brush. 'Hey Maddy, I've always wondered. Who did you have a crush on in primary school?'

'Yeah, who do you like, Maddy?' said Steph. She tucked her glasses back in under her towel turban. 'You never told us.'

'Nobody,' I said. I flicked through the pages of *Girlfriend*. Colour palettes ... horror stories ... how to know if your crush ... what kind of girlfriend ... how to be ... effortless ... oh my God ...

'You must have liked somebody before,' said Steph.

'We've told you all our crushes,' said Rachel. 'You've gotta give us something. It's only fair.'

'It can be a celebrity,' said Steph.

'I don't know any celebrities.'

'Is it a girl? We won't tell,' said Rachel.

'No, and I don't even know any boys. We go to an all-girls high school, remember.'

'Fine, but in primary school,' Rachel insisted. 'There's no reason not to tell us about primary school.'

The pause extended. I looked around, as if waiting for someone to tell me that it was okay, that my particular crush was not supposed to have happened for a year or so yet, and that, as I had always suspected, the others had only had crushes because they read so many *Girlfriend* magazines. It was a hobby for them to pick out boys and exaggerate their qualities.

I tried to think of who had been the most physically attractive of the boys from our Year Eight class. Half of them had been only as tall as our elbows back then and most had spent their free time banging their heads against the desks competitively.

'I guess I might have had a crush on Will, like, just a little bit.' Will had been tall with blond hair like a surfer, and good at sports, and kind of stoic like a sportsman should be. He was a solid choice.

'Maddy!' exclaimed Rachel, delighted. And then, inexplicably, she was angry. 'I can't believe you never told me.'

5

Sia Maulalo-Smith was the life of the party. She had a laugh like an open fire and a voice made for singing Beyoncé's 'Halo'. It was not really a party, but an old classroom with lasagne stuck to the ceiling. Even so, when Sia called me over the girls grouped around her fell silent. I was the audience member being invited onto the stage.

'Yep?' I said.

'Do you have a boyfriend?'

'Yeah,' I said, sarcastically, because of course I didn't.

'Oh? What's his name? How long have you been going out?'

It wasn't a joke. Sia and her friends had been making a tally of who had boyfriends and who didn't. When the hell did it happen, I wondered, that relationships stopped being outrageous and became a dimension of life like some sort of renovated attic in the Hauora house we'd learned about in health class, and everyone carrying on about it, like we were supposed to advertise for tenants?

'No,' I corrected her. 'I meant no; I don't have a boyfriend.'

'Oh,' she said, and I detected disappointment.

6

'Who do you like, Maddy? Who do you have a crush on?'

I was at home, at the dinner table, my two sisters and me in our school uniforms, and Dad, and Karen too who was visiting, and Mum in the kitchen, dishing out dessert with the special preserved Moorpark apricots, which was only because Karen was visiting and because we had begged and pleaded. I rolled my eyes, sighed and pulled my Bieber fringe across my eyes.

'Nobody,' I said. My sisters laughed.

Chrissy poked me and said, 'Sure, sure.' Her eyes narrowed slightly behind her glasses.

'But like, who have you liked in the past?' Britta said.

'Nobody.'

'Do you like girls?' Britta was not going to give up, now that she had picked up the scent of inconsistency.

'That's cool too,' said Chrissy.

'Yeah,' said Karen, 'you can tell us.'

'No. I don't like girls,' I said.

'Come on Mad, give us something,' said Dad in his teasing voice.

'Oh, leave her alone,' said Mum. 'She doesn't want to tell you.' I wanted to be grateful to mum for defending me, only I was annoyed, because she too had got it wrong. I didn't have anything to tell. I huffed. I could feel my silence becoming suspicious.

'Ooh, she has a secret crush,' said Britta.

'Maddy! Tell us,' said Chrissy.

I sighed a long, bored sigh to fill in time and show how much I didn't care.

'Not any of those high school idiots.' I said. 'I'm only into older guys. You know, university guys.'

'Maddy!' They all burst out laughing.

I hadn't met any university guys, so I couldn't prove myself wrong.

7

'Let's brainstorm some words that people might use to describe their sexuality or their sexual orientation. Just throw them at me,' the teacher said brightly, her green marker poised. 'Yes, Sydney.'

'Gay.'

'Yes. Good job.'

'Straight,' someone called out. Bisexual was next, and someone else offered pansexual.

'Good job. We can go through what these words mean in a minute. Anything else?' There was silence. 'Has anyone heard of asexuality?'

'Isn't that like aphids, Miss?' said Sydney.

'Yeah, we learned that in biology,' said her friend Alex. 'It's where they like, have sex with themselves and make clones.'

'It is a biological term,' said the teacher, 'but it means a different thing when we are talking about people. Asexual just means that you're not sexually attracted to anyone, regardless of gender.'

'Isn't that just like abstinence, Miss?'

'No. Abstinence is when you choose not to have sex even though you might be attracted to people, but asexuality is not a choice, it's just that some people just aren't interested to begin with. Good question, though. Any other terms anyone can think of?'

Nobody could think of any.

I wasn't *not* interested. I wanted to be interested. I wanted to be like everyone else. I was just a late bloomer. If I was that 'asexual' or whatever, I'd know. Although Miss did say not everyone knew, straight off, what they were. She didn't say *why* they wouldn't know, though. Some people just knew, and others mysteriously didn't. I couldn't have met enough guys yet to know whether I was attracted to any of them. Surely you had to meet a large variety before you knew. That was the problem with having an all-girls high school and no brothers to bring their friends around. Anyway, I couldn't be asexual. I wanted a relationship, with the Whirlwind Romance, with the losing your shoes and embracing in the rain and telling each other everything and being together forever like in the worst movie ever.

I put the term to the back of my mind and didn't think about it again—except for when I took a quiz at the end of the Health segment ('List six possible sexual orientations')— until I was twenty-two.

8

Clubbers filled Long Street, pressed body to body as they walked. The Uber slowed to walking pace, so we got out in the middle of the road and walked. Ian led, like a real British tourist in his khaki shorts and Mohammed the stuffed monkey swinging, stunned, from his backpack. I trailed behind with the girls—Steph and Kayla from the Midwest, and Diana from Romania. We all lived together and two more of our roommates were going to meet us at the club. It was only 11:30pm. I was twenty years old and we were going out to lose our inhibitions and thus experience life with its key components of listening to strangers tell you their stories of future business ventures and jumping up and down in more varied and daring ways than we had before.

It was that time of the evening when Cape Town was body temperature. In that temperature your personal inhibitions fail to kick in and very soon, especially if you are not used to it, the whole city becomes your living room and you are wandering around it half-dressed. Bodies converged on the street and cars were no longer understood to have right of way. Taxis and delivery vehicles stuck in the Saturday night flux tried to bully their way out with their horns at full blast, like lost tromboners after the marching band has moved on.

I was wearing the pale rose pencil skirt that clung to my legs so that I would move delicately, or so I thought. Actually the skirt hindered my movement and I knew the line of my underwear could be seen through the fabric by anyone looking closely. Every time I thought nobody was looking, I tugged the underwear straight again so that it was not denting the curve of my arse cheeks.

We filed into the Dubliner and our hands were stamped. We sifted through sticky bodies on our way to the bar and went upstairs with our pint glasses to the moshpit, where the lights flashed right down our throats and into our chests, pink and green and thudding. I had forgotten that Guinness tasted like Marmite. I had forgotten how much my ears would hurt. The confidence I had felt stepping out of the car began to drain out of me. I stuck close to the wooden pillars that divided the dance floor, but in a couple of minutes, with all the lights and thrusting elbows, I had lost everyone. I was not drunk enough to let go of my inhibitions, so I went down to the bar.

'Whiskey, on the rocks please,' I said.

'What kind of whiskey?' the bartender asked, gesturing to a black menu board covered in white cursive print. I tried to read all of it at once and then gave up, and singled one out that was just called Irish Whiskey. The bartender reached for a bottle.

'Hey, you like whiskey?' A man was next to me at the bar. I could feel his proximity, though he did not touch me. He was an Afrikaner, with brown glasses and a mousy mop of hair long enough to be tucked behind his ears. He was late thirties or forties; I couldn't tell. He looked like he owned a vineyard.

'Sure,' I said, even though I wasn't sure that I liked whiskey. It just seemed like the sort of thing one should order at an Irish bar in order to lose one's inhibitions.

'Where are you from?' he asked.

'New Zealand.'

'Oh, really?' he said, as if I'd told him the whiskey was aged in Cuban mahogany.

'And yourself?' I asked.

'Cederberg area,' he said. He said something else, possibly about his vineyard. I couldn't hear properly because of all the people crushing in on either side. I nodded and smiled. 'Can I get you another drink?' he asked.

He was probably a good guy, not even too old. How old was too old? What difference did it make? The thing is, I did not often go to clubs, because I hated clubbing. But here I was, in an Irish club in Cape Town, of all places. Why? Because I needed urgently to 'experience life', and because statistically speaking this was one of my best chances to begin a Whirlwind Romance in a Foreign City. Which was the first step to fixing my non-existent love life, which was my back-up plan in case my career failed. Since I hadn't yet seen anyone and felt magical feelings, I'd decided to be pro-active. You had to take what you were offered if you were serious about having a Whirlwind Romance in a Foreign City, otherwise you wouldn't get around to it. He was probably a nice guy. He did look like a serial rapist a little, but it was mainly the glasses. I hesitated.

'I'm sorry, I have to go find my friends,' I said.

He looked disappointed, and as I left up the stairs I felt guilty, as if I had been terribly rude.

In the moshpit, bodies. I drank the whiskey and left the glass on one of the wooden posts. I was so angry with myself that I decided to go berserk. I waded into the pit and became one of the pit people. We were like bats writhing from the dark wood, limbs waving, pressed together, the electric light displays shocking us blind and leaping through our skin.

Hands slid around my waist and held me there as I danced. They were hands the colour of the wood. A body pressed into my back, as I swayed, and began rubbing. A mouth started kissing my neck, and I could feel teeth. I thought, Am I going to let this happen?

The hands crept in and down my legs, so I grabbed them and moved them firmly back to my waist. But they moved in and down again. I yanked them away. They came back. I looked for an escape and, thank God, I could see the girls again. Through the tangle of limbs four or five of them were dancing together, facing each other.

A second guy was in front of me suddenly and he stuck

his hand to my crotch, pressing the fabric into the gap and grabbing, fast and deliberate like a tongue darting out of a mouth, then he disappeared behind some other people who were pushing past. The guy behind me was still holding me and sliding his hands down again, as if I wouldn't notice. I could see the other guy looking at me behind this tide of dancers. I forced the hands apart and shoved my way out, darting behind two girls' sequinned dresses. I tried to move but the crowd was pressing in on me, and he was following. One guy was between the girls and me, and one was behind me. They were coming at me through the crowd. They were a team, like hyenas closing in on their prey. The press of bodies was suffocating now and I couldn't move through it. The lights made the world flicker on and off. The drumbeat buzzed through my chest. I was almost there, but I could see that one of these men could make it to me first. I pushed my way through, pressing through elbows and hips, and there was a hand on my thigh. I pulled away. Turned around. They'd both reached me.

'Come on, bitch.'

'Hey, dance with me,' said the other one.

'No,' I said, turning away.

'Maddy, are you all right?'

It was Steph, her face a pale globe. I'd reached them, almost. They pushed their circle towards me.

Diana beckoned me in. 'Dance with us.'

I pushed my way into the circle, and the girls danced around me, forming a barricade. I looked back at the men, and one of them mouthed something like 'cunt'. His eyes in the dark were cream, like the flesh of a tinned pear.

'Are you okay?' The girls put their arms on my shoulders. I nodded and pretended to dance, and if anyone had seen, it would just be a bunch of girls dancing in a pit of other people dancing, with the blue light pulsing in your throat and the perfume of sweat and beer and perfume and powder rising in the steam of the bodies jumping up and down like waves and we are all underwater in all these bodies like seaweed, moving with the jump of the water and not a care where it touches.

After a while, I became very tired, and very sober. It was harder to jump in this way and not feel like sinking instead to the sticky floor. The hyenas were gone, I thought. I couldn't see them through the crowds, so I slipped away from the girls and out of the moshpit.

Ian wasn't around so I went down the stairs, dark wooden stairs with heavy doors to suffocate the sound, a staircase to breathe in. Ian wasn't the dancing type, so he might be ready to go home as well. But he wasn't downstairs. The crowd was less dense here and a band was setting up. I looked from one face to the next; not Ian, not Ian. Darker faces, glittery faces, older and fatter and skinnier faces. Every time I made eye contact with someone I recoiled. Something hostile in their eyes said, I don't know you. What are you looking at?

'Hey, girl, are you all right?' It was a stranger with glowing teeth.

'Yeah, just looking for my friends,' I said.

'Can I get you a drink?'

I sighed. I was going to say no, this was not a good time, but then I thought of the Whirlwind Romance.

He was relatively handsome, I supposed. Tall, dark, symmetrical, no major oddities or blemishes. I had to stop confusing people with predators. How was I supposed to have a romance if I assumed all people were untrustworthy?

'Sure,' I said. 'Thanks.'

'Here, sit down, I'll get you a drink. Then I help you look for your friends, okay?'

'Okay.' I was cool, this was cool, everything was cool.

'My name's Tendai.' He steered me to one of the corner tables. 'I'll get us some drinks. What would you like?'

'Just a beer, a light beer,' I said. 'Not a Guinness.'

He went to the bar. I unplugged a pint glass that was stuck to the table and watched people returning from the bar, ferrying drinks.

'Maddy!' I turned, and it was Ian, pint glass in hand. 'How's it going?'

I shrugged.

'You good?' he said.

I nodded. Before I could say anything else, Tendai returned with the beer. I took a sip. It was sweet, like fizzy drink.

'Where are the dutchies?' said Ian, his word for the two girls from the Netherlands. They'd been dancing with Steph and Kayla.

'Upstairs, I think,' I said.

'Wait here. I'll be back.'

I wanted to say stop, wait, don't go. But I didn't have a good enough reason.

'He is your friend?' asked Tendai, as Ian left.

'Yes,' I said.

'Ah, see—I tell you we find them.'

I found myself looking at the door swinging shut.

'Where are you from?' he was saying.

'New Zealand,' I said, and I couldn't hear his response. 'Where are you from?'

'Zimbabwe.'

'Oh, cool. What brings you to Cape Town?'

'I come here for business,' he said.

'What do you do?'

'I am driving bus, uh, tour guide. But I am here in Cape Town on my own business.'

'Oh, what business?'

'I am selling, how do you say? Art, artwork, made of stone.'

'Sculpture?'

'Uh, yes, do you want to see?'

He brought up his old flip phone and showed me a picture of a stone chair shaped like a lion. It was outside on the grass and some kids were standing around it, staring dead-eyed.

'Did you make it?' I asked.

'No, a friend make it and I sell it for him.'

I felt his hand on my leg. I didn't move it. I thought about moving it, and walking away, but I didn't.

Then he leaned across the table and kissed me. His mouth tasted like the inside of a mouth. Not repulsive, exactly. I let him keep going, hoping the romance aspect would kick in if I tried hard enough, like a dial-up internet connection.

I could see Ian in my peripheral vision. I wondered when the kissing would stop naturally, because I was a little bored and uncomfortable. But my first instinct was to be polite. After all, the guy had bought me a beer. I wanted to send a secret distress signal to Ian, so he could save me somehow. If only there was a secret hand signal. Ian sat down. I broke away rather forcefully then, with the excuse of turning to Ian and saying, 'Hi.' I took a sip of beer, and another sip of beer because I couldn't make out with anyone if I was sipping. 'Did you find them?'

'Yeah. Are you okay?'

'Mm hmm.' I sipped more beer.

'Come with me,' said Tendai, shuffling closer to whisper in my ear. It tickled. I didn't turn to look at him. 'We'll get a hotel room.'

Now I knew how stupid I had been. It all felt the same as that guy who had grabbed me in the moshpit, only this time it was my own fault. I had played tricks on my own mind, thinking this was a good idea. 'No, thanks,' I said.

'Can we go to your place?'

'No, I'm not allowed.' It was a believable sort of rule, I thought.

'Okay, just please let's talk, through there.' He pointed to a corridor across from us.

'Where?'

'In the toilets,' he said, and he seemed to not want to say the word.

'No,' I said.

'They're clean,' he added. 'Please.'

I made a face to Ian, no longer caring if Tendai could see the face.

'Do you wanna go?' Ian mouthed at me.

I nodded. 'I have to go now,' I said to Tendai.

He pleaded with me, and in the end I gave him my number, as I was a generous person and didn't want to seem rude.

We stepped outside, and the world seemed to expand.

'Sorry,' I said, laughing. 'I can't go back in that club now.'

'It's not easy, is it,' said Ian. 'Do you wanna go home now, or do you wanna go to the bar across the road?'

'Yes, yes, let's go there. God, I'm so stupid.'

The street was clear and fizzing. A beerish light spilled into all the little holes in the road and caught in the sparkly silver purse of a girl stepping into her taxi.

The bar across the road had a hallway dark as the entrance to a museum. A man held out a stamp for our hands.

'Whoops,' I said, almost tripping over the step.

'It's not easy, is it Maddy,' Ian slurred. It was a verbal tic of his. 'I'm having a vodka 'n coke. Do you wanna vodka 'n coke, Maddy?'

'Yes, please. I think I'm drunker than I thought.'

We were in a sort of octagonal space with a bar on one corner. I was close to the floor. Time and people jumbled and the light was making patterns on the floor like giant thumbprints in purple or gold, and I had half a vodka and coke left.

'Drink this, please,' I said to Ian. 'I'll get vomity.'

'It's not easy, is it,' said Ian, and downed the lot. Then he bought three beers 'for the ride home', which were all, as per the bar's policy, opened for him at the bar. 'Let's go home, shall we?' he said. We called an Uber.

The Uber was warm and new inside except for the spilt beer at Ian's feet. It was so good to be on our way, with the lights and the harbour outside, and the base of Table Mountain where the zebras were sleeping, and us in the soundproofed interior speeding home.

'What did you think of that guy I was making out with before?' I asked Ian.

'I thought he was a prat. I could tell you weren't really into it, but you put up with it for some reason.'

'Ugh. Men. I mean, not you, but men. They're always hitting on you.'

'Maddy, I promise,' said Ian. 'I will never hit on you.'

9

I didn't tell my writing group what this essay was about before they read it. I made them promise not to read ahead in case they found out what it was about in a way I couldn't control.

They read the essay and when we met again, many positive things were said, which I ignored because this information didn't feel crucial to my survival.

Then one of them said, 'So Ian, eh? I wondered if he was the one you found you were attracted to after all?'

'No,' I said frustratedly, even though workshop etiquette dictated the author should not speak during the workshop or try to explain what they had meant.

Someone else said, 'That section in the bar, it felt so excruciatingly naïve, it was hard to read.'

'It felt like watching a car crash you could do nothing about,' another person agreed.

I said nothing. I felt my blood becoming cold and slow inside me. I sat very still as if I might shatter.

Many more nice things were said, which I immediately forgot. After the workshop, I went to the apartment I was paid to clean and took six hours to do a job that should have taken two. I lay on the couch in the apartment, trying to thaw. Finally, I became angry and I began to ask myself why I was angry. I articulated the reason in my head over and over until

I could have explained it to a live studio audience in the future when I was famous from publishing a collection of personal essays that had captured the public imagination, gained a cult following worldwide and won the Booker Prize, an amazing feat, since it wasn't even a novel so shouldn't have qualified.

'So, this Ian character,' the TV presenter said, 'some people have been shipping you two. Was there a spark there?'

'No,' I laughed. 'I wasn't into Ian. I'm sorry, but he's not the one who's going to turn me normal. And I'd just like to point out that it is possible for two people of the opposite gender to have concern for each other without also fucking.'

'So true.' The presenter nodded as the audience applauded. 'So, so true. Can I ask one more question? I've picked one at random from our Twitter feed. This is from Caitlyn from Montana. She says, "The scene in the bar felt like watching a car crash I could do nothing about. You seemed very naïve ..."' The presenter paused. 'Oh, I thought she was going to follow with a question but that's the whole question. Could you respond to that statement?'

'Not a problem,' I said. 'Yes, I was naïve. Or, I am still naïve. But also, it's more complicated than that. There are the things that you *know*. For example, you don't have to do anything you don't want to. Then there are the things you subconsciously believe, such as, be polite. Be kind. Sexual attraction is something that will happen to you if you try hard enough, and this idea that sexual attraction is something that everyone has, therefore, you have it, therefore, any physical sensation in your body—the shock of a strange hand on the knee—is a sign to continue. Look, some people have the ability to make decisions in crowded bars that integrate their conscious knowledge and recognise their false subconscious beliefs for what they are. Other people are naïve.'

10

On the last weekend of my stay in South Africa, I participated in a Whirlwind Romance. He was a business major from Cameroon who wore a cowboy hat to our first and only date, on the night before my plane left. I thought the cowboy hat was genre-appropriate. I thought things were going well. He spoke in a soothing growl. I made careful calculations as I drank all of the expensive whiskey in his apartment. I didn't actually want to sleep with him, but time was of the essence. And wasn't it said that you'll like it when you try it? I'd already tried it and hadn't liked it, but they also said about broccoli that you have to try it at least ten times before you'll like it. Who was it who actually said that? I couldn't remember. It seemed like solid advice.

And I thought I'd figured out attraction. It was the kind of warmth of wanting someone to continue talking to you in their low soothing growl. Insofar as I was aware at this point, attraction was an all-or-nothing phenomenon. It was either there or it wasn't. And, if it was, if you were attracted to someone, then logically you must enjoy sex with them. That's what I thought.

Afterwards, I said, 'Yes, it was painful, but I don't have much experience, so it's to be expected.'

'Stay here in Cape Town,' the business major said, and gave me a blue handmade bracelet. But I took a taxi to my flat at 2am. All of my belongings were strewn across the floor and covered in a fine layer of desert sand. My plane was due to leave in a few hours.

Weeks later he Skyped me. 'Meet me in Italy,' he said. I looked away from the screen and ripped the piece of paper I was holding into small flakes like snow.

11

It's like this. You are twenty-two. So far, you have assumed that these stories about sexual attraction are an exaggeration, a kind of cultural conceit which transcends genre, infiltrating not just literature but movies, television, music and most teenage conversations. The woman sees the man across the room on the first day of her new job. He flicks his hair in a dashing way. The woman's heart rate increases. Blood rushes downwards, doing strange things to her genitalia. She stops thinking coherently. This kind of reaction is called love at first sight, which you can either believe in or not. You haven't questioned the centrality of this myth, or the fact that everyone your own age seems obsessed with sex and wants to have mundane conversations about it and compare the body parts of strangers, until one day you do question it. You remember health class at high school, and how you'd expected it to start making sense at some point in the future, only it hadn't.

You have to google a whole lot of ridiculous-sounding questions you don't really believe are legitimate, like, 'How many people should I sleep with to make sure I'm not straight? What actually is sexual attraction? How often are normal people attracted to other people?' All of that gets more and more confusing, until finally you just google 'What sexuality am I?' All of this takes time out of your busy schedule and makes you feel very stupid. If only there was a handy quiz like they'd made you do in high school to figure out your career and it had said you should be an architect, and that was that. Except that you hated maths, and the one time you built something, you really just stood around pretending to be interested while other people built it for you, because things fitting together in space made you want to say screw space, and gravity, and structural integrity, and float up into the sky out of pure defiance. But, in theory, you love quizzes.

It turns out there is a quiz. The quiz asks you, 'Are you mostly attracted to men, women, or sometimes one and sometimes the other?' But what does 'attracted to' mean, you want to ask. How often should it happen? Towards what proportion of men or women? With what degree of intensity?

And you start to wonder if you really could have been attracted to the business major with the cowboy hat since you hadn't actually wanted to have sex with him at all.

You start to wonder whether you were to some degree attracted to that blond girl because of that time when she was leaving the country and you were so drunk and sad you both fell on the floor during the hug.

You start to wonder if you were attracted to that boy who pestered you till you let him pay you for a hug.

You substitute people for dog versions of those people and, in many cases, you much prefer the dog versions of people.

At some point you come across the word *asexual* and you think, no.

You don't want to be that.

You just don't want to. Asexuality is so unsexy. You think you know what sexy means, because you've always wanted to be it.

You've never met anyone who's openly asexual. You try to imagine an asexual person and you imagine a lonely weirdo who lives in their parents' garage, dyes their hair purple to make a statement, or dresses like an alien, like that person in New York you heard about on the internet who had surgery to make themself look like an alien, and who wanted no penis but no vagina either, just nothing.

Or you imagine a nun who won't look at herself when she showers, or Kerewin from *The Bone People* who lives on her own in a tower. You remember seeing some people in a Pride parade once, and thinking, oh yeah, they exist, and then thinking no more about it. You hate parades.

You find a YouTube clip of three girls sitting down to rest after marching in a Pride parade. A guy approaches them with a camera, all professionally got up.

'Oh, you gotta be kidding me,' he says when he sees their signs. 'Asexuals?'

The group try to politely explain what asexuality is, but he just shakes his head pityingly and for fifteen minutes, with a patronising smirk, he becomes an unsolicited counsellor. 'You must be so sad and lonely. If you don't have sex, how can you be a well-balanced person? What do you do with your time? It seems like you've just never experienced the physical connection, the chemistry to really wanna be with someone on a physical spiritual level. You haven't encountered that person yet. I have met several women who I was spiritually, emotionally, physically attracted to, and sex is just the pinnacle of that. Come on, ladies, come on. I hope you make it there. To sit there with this sign, it's a cry for help. What happened to you guys? Don't you have a dildo or something? I'm not trying to be an arsehole, I'm not. I'm being an adult, let's be adults. I don't judge you guys; I just feel bad for you.'

For a moment, you think you recognise this guy. Then you realise it's just his ideas that are familiar. He's the voice in your head made manifest.

As you continue your research, you find out that almost all of the conversations about asexuality in the world are happening on one forum called AVEN. One thing you can't stand, almost as much as you can't stand marching in a parade, is participating in a forum. People on AVEN tend to be on journeys to understand themselves better. It's understandable, but you don't really want to join them, as one thing you dislike more than forums, and maybe on par with your dislike of parades, is going on a personal journey. A personal journey is a bitch because it takes you by surprise. You never know when you're beginning it and then suddenly you're writing a personal essay collection.

You don't want to be a forum person. In any case, you have boring aspirations: to meet an intelligent, funny person who falls in love with you, can't live without you, has you at the centre of their dream, too; it's a dream of being a dream. The dream of throwing a glorified party and gaining the approval of your more religious relatives. The dream of being, and having, a plus-one at events for evermore. Holidays in Tokelau, and one manageable child who will grow up to be the prime minister.

On the forums, you find out that there are different types of attraction. Many people experience these types of attraction all at once; the attractions can be tightly woven, indistinguishable from one another. But when one type of attraction is missing, like a loose piece of thread, suddenly you can get your fingers into the fabric and separate out the strands. Sex drive is different from sexual attraction, is different from sensual attraction, is different from romantic attraction, is different from aesthetic attraction. This means that you can be asexual and still be romantically attracted to someone. You can even be asexual and still have sex. Theoretically, you can be asexual and still *want* sex, so long as that desire is not directed towards a specific person; i.e. you can still have a sex drive. It's one thing to understand that asexuality means you have never been sexually attracted to anyone, but another thing to understand that that might be *all* it means (although some people identify as asexual for other reasons, such as a lack of libido or sex-repulsion, and this is legitimate also).

You realise you might have been confusing romantic, sensual and even aesthetic attraction for sexual attraction, because you didn't know what it was.

Like Noah on his ark, popping up to the top deck to check if the bird has returned with signs of life, you search for news of asexuality on the public news pages. Mostly, 'asexual' is used as an insult to describe people who are not necessarily asexual. Or a word that's included in a list of types to illustrate diversity.

One article mentions a book called *Understanding Asexuality* by Anthony Bogaert. You look it up. It's not written by an asexual person but an academic. You don't want to read it because you might belong to the category 'asexual'. You don't want to read it because you might not belong.

The only representation of an out asexual that you can find in pop culture is in a recent Netflix cartoon called *Bojack Horseman*, which is about a depressed horse. In season four, one of the main characters, Todd, comes out as asexual. Many people on the forums are ecstatic about this, but you don't really care. Todd isn't really anything like you.

In the Ace community, some people are jokingly called 'unassailable asexuals' or 'ideal asexuals'. They are called this because they lack all of the traits that are often blamed for asexuality, so they make good spokespeople. They are healthy, extroverted and physically attractive, and they have never experienced abuse or assault. They don't appear naïve. They also don't have a libido and are aromantic, so you don't have to understand the different types of attraction in order to accept that they're asexual. More complicatedly asexual people, on the other hand, are often dismissed by the general public with an eyeroll. 'Demi-panromantic auto-chorissexual? Gyneromantic grey bisexual? What will they come up with next?'

12

For much of human history, people pretended that asexuality didn't exist. Then, for some time, people pretended that all women were asexuals. Then feminism happened, and no one was asexual anymore. Women were free from oppression, which meant free to express our true sexual nature.

In 1994, British researchers were trying new approaches to tackling the AIDS epidemic. They needed to help physicians identify those most at risk, so they carried out a survey with 18,000 participants to find out about sexual attitudes and behaviours. One of the questions asked participants to complete the statement 'I have been sexually attracted to . . .' with one of six options. The first five options included 'only females', 'only males', mostly one or the other, or both. The sixth option read, 'I have never felt sexually attracted to anyone at all.'

One per cent of the respondents picked option six. This was about the same number as those who reported being same-sex attracted. The data from this one question on this survey is still generally considered to be the best estimate for the global prevalence of asexuality we have today.

In New Zealand, a 2017 survey asked the open-ended question 'How would you describe your sexual orientation?' Only 0.2 per cent answered by writing 'asexual'. It may not seem like many, but it's a much more specific question than that of the 1994 survey: it assumes that the respondent has the vocabulary and knowledge to describe their sexual orientation, an assumption which proved, to some degree, false. 13.3 per cent either stated their refusal to answer or left a blank, and 9.5 per cent answered in a way which indicated they did not understand the term 'orientation'. Among these responses were 'waning with age', 'concluded', 'none', 'haven't had it for ages (lol)', 'female', 'dull', 'five stars', 'wellbeing', 'European', 'haha', 'oral???:-)', 'disorientated', and 'what?????'

Even some heterosexuals seemed not to entirely under-stand the question: 9.4 per cent of respondents indicated they were heterosexual by answering with variations of 'normal', 'completely normal', and 'not sure what you mean by this—normal'. Another 0.3 per cent simply stated that they were *not* gay, and another 1.6 per cent described their heterosexuality in other ways like 'man marry woman', or 'I like vaginas'. Reading these responses feels a bit like reading an acrostic poem that a confused teenager has scratched into their desk with a compass.

13

Last week I met my sister in a café and she said that, when she was seven, her friends asked her who her crush was, and they said she had to have a crush, but she didn't, so she made one up. I was happy for a moment, as I knew we had experienced the same scenario, only I'd been fourteen when it happened to me.

'I've never had a crush,' I said.

'That feels like a lie,' she said.

'Well, you would say that,' I said, batting it away.

That feels like a lie kept flashing in my mind after that and I couldn't get it out. I did wonder if, after all, I'd imagined it. If I'm repressing something. If this whole essay is a complicated feat of justification for something I've done wrong.

14

Think of it this way. You're a horse but you live in the Namib Desert and all your friends are oryx. You think of yourself as a deformed oryx. What else could you be? You live in a habitat that doesn't accommodate horses. You've been seeing a gap above your head for as long as you can remember. You've grown up being told stories about how great it is to charge through the open desert, spearing enemies with two pointy horns. You don't yet have the vocabulary to understand that a gap is an illusion; you see it only when you picture what it isn't.

Adventure Time

'Are you excited about university life, Madison?'

The assistant principal was as tall as my elbow, a scarf around her neck like a girl scout. She smiled her assistant-principal smile. I was so accustomed to seeing that smile used as a shield against teenage Goliaths that for a moment I felt as though I were in detention again.

'Yes.' I smiled back. After all, we were almost equals now, drinking cups of tea while surrounded by celebratory variations of salmon and cream cheese sandwiches wrapped in flax bows or breadless and speared with little sticks, with olives on top. 'I'm looking forward to it,' I said, sucking an olive off a toothpick. 'I'm going to burn a couch down.'

'I don't think that's a good idea,' she said.

I grew my smile to match hers. I felt as if I were a chosen one about to embark on a pre-ordained adventure.

'I think it's a great idea, a rite of passage.'

'You don't really mean that.' She expected me to cave then, but I was used to thwarting her.

'Yes, I do,' I said. 'I'm going to burn a couch on Castle Street.'

*

Café LOL was filled with a shadowless kind of light resembling a sitcom. The backlit red display case behind the kitchen showcased an array of empty vases. Nearby, some thirteen-year-olds were ironically riding a pair of featureless, primary-coloured rocking horses in the children's play area and taking selfies. Riley looked uncomfortable hunched on the other side of the table.

I sipped my hot chocolate as Riley relayed to Liv the latest from their group home. Liv had just moved out. Someone had swallowed a razor again, or was it that they had overdosed, and the razor was an old story? I wasn't following. The group home was for kids whose parents didn't know how to handle them, or that's how Liv explained it. She had hated it, she said, because they had confiscated all the hair straighteners. Her hair was much better curly anyway, I thought. It was kind of lifeless now that she had regained her hair straightener. It kept falling over her eyes like a blackout curtain.

Liv and Riley had fallen silent, and Riley looked at me uncertainly. She and I were supposed to be getting to know each other so that I could decide if I wanted her to be our third flatmate. She wasn't what I had expected. She had the physique of a malnourished child, with long mousy hair that looked as if it were there to keep her warm.

We had already signed the lease on a three-bedroom in the North East Valley and had a few weeks before we were supposed to move in.

'Boobs,' said Riley, to break the silence.

'Titties,' said Liv.

I cleared my throat. 'All right,' I said. 'It's time for your flatmate test.'

'Test?' said Riley. 'Jesus H. Christ.'

Liv snickered. I unfolded a serviette to reveal a scrawling bullet-pointed list and clicked my pen. I had copied down all the questions from the flashback episode of *The Big Bang Theory* where Sheldon interviews his prospective roommate Leonard. I had an idea that I would be the Sheldon Cooper of this flat. It would be just like the flat in *The Big Bang Theory* too, with in-jokes and enemies and adventures and everyone figuring out that whole 'romance' thing together.

'What is the sixth noble gas?' I asked.

'Er,' said Riley. 'Let me think. Elements ... hydrogen, helium, lithium, beryllium, boron. Boron? Is boron a gas?'

'No,' I said, writing a cross on my serviette. 'The sixth *noble gas* is radon. Next question: What time do you evacuate your bowels?'

*

Liv and Riley had been living in the flat for a week, but there were no lights on when I arrived. Riley was hugging her knees and sucking her hair in the middle of the big dirty cream carpet. Liv was kneeling, with her back in a large green bucket.

'Hello Maddy,' she said, waving her hand out of the bucket. 'I'm a turtle.'

The flat had the feel and smell of an empty coolroom at the back of a grocery store.

'Why is there no furniture?' I asked.

'We have a chair,' said Liv, pointing to what looked like a large beach ball. 'Also, sorry, there's no electricity yet. I'm sorting it out tomorrow, but I have to go to the library to get internet.'

'You've been living here for a week!' I said.

I turned the beach ball over and found that it was a blow-up armchair. I sat down in it, wobbling. On the far side of the room, a bowl of cold miso soup was reflecting the dim porchlight from the window. Beyond that, everything was black.

'I want to be a turtle,' I said.

*

My lecture halls were vast and identical to one another on the inside. Hundreds of students converged in the rows and opened their laptops. From the back row I could see all the screens, like the windows of a high rise if you were to dangle yourself out of the top floor and look down. My psychology professors talked about significance and cognition, and tests where people were brought into a room with paid actors and asked which line was longer. Each 'naïve participant' claimed that the two lines shown on the screen were the same length, because the actors had said so and the participant wanted to fit in. But the lines weren't the same length. The professors said that maybe this was human nature, that we could all so easily become Nazis.

*

When I walked home through the gardens, the trees reached through the purple dark among ghost-pale roses. Often it rained heavily, and the wind groaned. Everything slowed down around me, my limbs becoming one with the water, flowing out into the trees which thrashed, twisting in their beds like epileptics.

Walking through the door I'd find my flat the same as I had left it in the morning. The glass blender I had dropped weeks ago was laid out in shards on the side table, waiting to be disposed of. The bunch of pale yellow parsley remained in yellow water on the sill. The dishes had to be scraped clean of old food in cold water before we could use the cutlery. But our brand new textbooks remained centre-stage on the coffee table, symbols of our good intentions. We would flick through Liv's anatomy textbook, in awe of the detailed webs of colour-coded and named blood vessels.

Liv's mother had given us a spice rack stacked with every spice we'd ever heard of, so we imagined cooking things with star anise and bay leaves. My mother gave us a herb garden and a little pumpkin plant, which Liv was very excited about and watered regularly. We revelled in these gifts, each an expectation for the expansion of our lives, for the new chapter. But left to ourselves, each day felt large and cold. Liv, having downloaded cartoons onto a hard-drive and Pokémon and Minecraft onto her laptop, slowly became nocturnal. She slept till late afternoon, got high, watched cartoons till 3am and slept again. Sometimes she didn't eat, and we had to bribe her, saying, 'Twelve more pieces of pasta and you can watch *Adventure Time*.' She became slow, seeming to conserve her energy, like a sloth. Riley liked to sit on the floor and rock herself. Between us, conversation was often thin on the ground. Liv and Riley sometimes burst into discussion about boobs, to break up moments of silence. I found this strange and annoying. I couldn't fathom what they got out of talking about them, since it seemed like more of a hands-on kind of interest.

I invited Liv and Riley to my parents' place for dinner one Sunday. Both of them, Riley especially, seemed slightly uncomfortable with my family's loud philosophical arguments around the dinner table, our open weirdness, the way we interrupted one another. They shrank, sending each other shy glances, although it could just have been the strangeness of being at anyone else's home. Everything familiar to me must be alien to someone else, I realised. I whispered 'Sorry' when they were introduced to my family's practice of holding hands during grace. I thought for sure they'd be weirded out by my parents' religiosity.

'Maddy, your family are awesome,' said Riley afterwards.

'Yeah, my family never talk about politics or psychology or anything,' said Liv.

'Mine don't really talk at all,' said Riley. 'We just shout at each other across the room.'

One day Marco appeared with Liv, and after that he seemed to be always at the flat. He looked like a young Allen Ginsberg, but with big ears and a supermarket uniform. On our little whiteboard, on which we had planned to write flat messages, he drew a penis. The whiteboard was cheap and the penis couldn't be washed off, and for whatever reason, apathy or our vague hope of being subversive, we never tried to remove it.

Marco brought Liv to life the way no one else could. He

could talk his way through any psychological conundrum I had learned in class, proving me wrong all the way back to the conception of the universe. I didn't have the skill to beat him at this game. Marco didn't care about the truth. He cared about winning arguments.

'I discovered at an early age that if I talked long enough, I could make anything right or wrong,' said Marco. He was quoting a phony lawyer from the TV show *Community*. 'So either I'm God or truth is relative.'

Liv eventually dropped out of uni. Her textbooks remained in the same place on the coffee table until we had to prise them off where they'd glued themselves down with spilt bong-water. She had collected a seedling and started growing a new plant, which she kept in the hot-water cupboard and took out from time to time to examine, water, and move from windowsill to windowsill, letting the sun soak into its new leaves, counting each new bud, excited not for the amount of weed it could produce when the leaves were dried, but the thrill of seeing it thrive under her care.

*

They were out on the back porch when I arrived home late one night. I could hear them laughing and muttering through the wall, like children misbehaving during a prayer. I turned the light off and walked out to them. The dark swirled, sparking the way it does when you come out of the light too fast. It was cold. The porch was suspended over the dense black of the communal grass, where trash had been thrown from apartment windows. The little fire burning at the end of the joint glowed orange against Riley's chin as she toked and passed it along. Liv's hair flicked forward into a spark and it looked for a second like she would burst into flames.

'Maddy!' said Marco, smiling. 'Maddy's here.'

'Hi, Maddy,' the others said.

'Oh wait, uh, this is a cigarette,' said Marco.

'She's not stupid, Marc,' said Liv.

'Maddy, do you want to try it?' said Riley.

'I feel like we're offering drugs to children,' said Marco.

'I'm only a few months younger than you,' I said. I resented being the only one who was still seventeen. I sat down and took the joint in my fingers.

'Just hold it in your mouth and then breathe it out,' Liv instructed. 'Don't swallow it.'

'Whatever you do, don't swallow it,' said Marco.

It was like sucking up fire. I blew out into the sky. It was a clear indigo sky and I soon began to see more layers of it, the stars carrying on forever. They started to spin dizzily, spiralling gently outward into a universe so big my eyes could not contain it.

*

The next time I tried, I swallowed the smoke and felt nauseous, closed my eyes and found myself spiralling in and down like something heavy going down a drain. Even when I smoked it right, my memory disappeared for three seconds at a time, and I didn't like being stuck that way, unable to think. I saw the map of the world around me. Further to the south I saw my past being played out at my old house and my old school. I looked north towards the present and saw myself there on the porch, as if I was studying a painting from a different era.

Mostly I stayed inside on the couch with my blanket and coat on and wrote in my notebook. I wrote about the trees I had seen on the way home, the colours of the grass and the sky, the shadows; the way they had lain across the grass in slats, or swayed; the way the birds had danced and what they were squalling about, or what had made them lift off the supermarket roof like leaves in a gale, settling instead in the dark mess of trees. The only things I couldn't describe were my feelings. Everything was cold and slipping past me like silk.

*

'Don't think,' said Rochelle, 'just let go. But hold your legs stiff,' she added.

The material cinched my waist like a corset, looped around and under my legs and suspended me from the ceiling. A fountain of red silk spilled out of my clenched fists.

'I don't want to,' I said. I was surprised by the fear that held me there, clutching my silk near the ceiling beam.

'Only one way down,' said Rochelle, grinning.

I considered staying up in the rafters forever. Below, some of the dancers were inching painfully up like snails, cupping the silk with their feet, others rolling upward in spirals, backs curving, toes pointing, wrapping themselves in complex knots. I could see out the high windows at the rain pressing in. Up there with the weather, I felt like a secret military parachuter, about to drop. I imagined how fast I would go. My skull would hit the wood with a crack. My spine would splinter. I had thought courage was a matter of convincing myself of the logic that letting myself fall would not result in my death. But the logic couldn't breach the feeling. Here I was, and there was death, and still I had to fall, which was, in one mind, to give up life for a split second. I let go and dropped.

I yanked to a halt at the end of my plummet, my head a few feet from the mat. I untangled my legs ungracefully and lay down on the mat, feeling my heartbeat and the ache in my fingers and thighs. I peeled apart my fingers which stuck to each other with rosin and watched the dancers sleepily from my mattress. I liked to watch them as they swung and laughed and invented new tricks. Rochelle had messed up a roll-down and was doing a little tap-dance in the air as a finishing flourish to her fall. I wanted to be home in my room, watching *Game of Thrones* in the dark. But also, I didn't. It was healthy and good, being here, with all these people, with my muscles aching and my skin sticking to the hard plastic of the mattress and my breathing so large, and the raw bruises under my knees from where the silk had slipped, which I felt from time to time, like badges.

*

It was as if I was seeing the field through a spider's web. The motorway lights in the distance were a string of yellow beads. I tried to bat off the mist with my free hand, my cellphone hand pressed against my chest. My skin bristled. I told myself to adjust. Breathe, relax your muscles, become comfortable with the space around you.

We were walking to the pizza shop. I was wearing the Egyptian blue leotard and the see-through skirt, the one that fell forever against my freshly shaved legs like the tide. My feet were bare and if I stepped quickly enough they almost seemed to float.

I closed my eyes and ran into the pulsing blackness. It was a trick I had learned from a theatre class to destroy inhibitions. There is no cheaper or healthier thrill than running with your eyes closed.

After a certain distance, though, I stopped, opened my eyes and found Liv and Marco plodding along behind me. I helicoptered back to them. They were slow, tripping over the milky grass, their eyelids heavy. And he was explaining the way things were again. 'No Liv, Livvy, the government *want* us to think that. It's a game, don't you see, you're losing the game!'

Liv smiled and laughed because she didn't mind losing the game. I ran back a little way to check if it was her real smile. Sometimes I couldn't tell the difference between her real smile and the defensive one she used when she really wanted to stop talking and go back to bed. Satisfied that it was real, I turned again into the dense beard of mist and closed my eyes.

Breathe.

Relax your muscles.

Become comfortable with the space around you.

'Maddy's wearing lingerie,' came Marco's voice from behind me. 'Maddy, why are you wearing just lingerie?'

I turned around. In certain lights Marco's unruly black hair made him look like Harry Potter, with a secret joke in his eyes, as though he belonged to a world you couldn't see.

'I'm not,' I said.

He giggled as they approached with the stench of weed and tobacco. 'You're wearing a one-piece.'

'This is a leotard.' I rolled my eyes.

'What's a leer . . . turd?'

'It's what I wear for aerial silks.' I had to cover my arms to the elbow so I didn't get silk-burn on my under-arms, like the one on my palm. I stroked it with my thumb. The leathery scab felt like a kind of armour.

'Maddy,' he said, 'I'm sorry to destroy your innocence.'

'I'm not innocent. It's sportswear.' I wanted desperately not to be innocent.

'Maddy, I'm sorry but it's a one-piece, it's lingerie. And'— he cupped his mouth and whispered into the open air—'it's really hot.'

I kept my face blank, in a permanent eyeroll, and turned forward into the dark. The motorway curving around the paddock held it in a pocket of sound, so you could tell with your eyes closed where the edges were. I ran blindly, holding my arms in front of my face to deflect the obstacles I imagined might appear suddenly before me.

'It's really hot,' he said in a louder voice, and I guess Liv elbowed him in the gut then, as I heard him yelp.

'It's not lingerie, it's a leotard,' I shouted back, turning again to wait for them to approach. I needed him to understand the technical and intentional difference between the two.

'Women's lingerie is designed with a purpose,' he said, 'and that is to make my dick feel a certain way, okay. I don't know how to say this, but my dick knows that you're wearing lingerie.'

'Ew,' said Liv.

'That's very sexist,' I said, satisfied, as if I had just labelled an exotic fruit.

'It's the system that's sexist, Maddy. I'm just one dick wanting what a dick wants.'

There was a gap in the traffic, as there was occasionally at night. For a few seconds, no new cars entered Dunedin from the north and for much less than that, I looked in his eyes and it felt like something in me was being known that I didn't want known. It was a sick feeling, like warm fizzy drink.

'Bye,' I said, because apart from eyerolling it was the only way I knew how to respond.

I forced my arms down by my sides and charged through each phantom barrier without defences, proving that it was a ghost. Ghost! Ghost! Another ghost!

I heard Marco call after me again. 'Can I tell you a secret?' he said. I turned back, hands on hips, making sure to look bored.

'What?'

He beckoned, but I stayed where I was until he was close again.

He leaned in, so I could feel his hot breath on my ear. 'You're really pretty.'

He was watching me, and I was conscious of how my shoulders moved as I walked away, trying to make them express how much I didn't care.

I ran ahead. If I screamed loud enough in my mind I wouldn't be able to hear my own thoughts. He had read my mind, probably; he knew how dim and innocent I was, probably; everyone was probably laughing as I turned away.

bye

bye

I screamed until I drove all the thoughts back, screamed like I never would out loud, the kind of shriek that would be inappropriate at a death metal concert. I ran into the darkness, skimming over the surface of the grass like a ghost. In my head the scream made everything hot and black, and then somehow I changed the subject, thinking so fast—*I wonder what pizza I will buy when we get to Dominoes; Cheesy Garlic or Veg Trio, even though Veg Trio has only two vegetables because mushroom isn't a vegetable?*

Bye.

Not fast enough. It was all coming back.

When I opened my eyes, I saw the lamps at the edge of the highway. Light pooled on the grass like orange juice. The darkness would be even darker beyond the skeleton trees, behind the lights. I imagined myself in the Botanic Gardens across the motorway, among the trees, as close as bodies on the bus, but cool and damp and bony and eyeless; and the rhododendrons, pale flocks of them in the dark; and the underskirts of the trees, the cool damp foliage crawling over my leotard.

*

Many people came to the flat. They came at odd times, stayed for a few hours and then left again, sometimes in groups, sometimes alone. There was Leah, who declared that she never wore underwear, not even under jeans, and Ryan, who clutched the spliff gratefully when it was offered, who talked about loneliness and the strange dreams he had during frosts, and Caleb who cried because his girlfriend had left him and who baked apple syrup pastries for everyone, asking, 'Do you like them?' And then eating one himself and crying again because he thought it tasted like ashes. There was Nathan, who wore a Pikachu onesie, and Niko, who performed knife tricks on amphetamines as we watched in thrilled silence.

There was mescaline, which came in a horrible yellow pus, and mushrooms you could pick if you knew where, but they were always covered in sand, and you couldn't wash them if you wanted the effect. Everyone dreamed of trying DMT. People had taken it and been changed forever. They had felt themselves transform into trees, their skin turning to bark, their senses expanding as the wind threaded through the fingertips of their leaves, their brains growing slow and deciduous, thoughts falling to their feet, leaving their minds clean.

*

I heard Liv and Riley whispering when I came home. I followed their voices into Liv's room.

'Argh! Jesus H. Christ,' whispered Riley loudly.

Liv laughed. 'We didn't hear you come in.'

'What's going on?' Sitting down on the carpet with them, I saw my mother's Happy Chicken soup bowl covered in dried noodles.

'Sorry, but we're tripping balls here,' said Riley. She started laughing silently, as if on mute.

'There are angry people with threatening forearms after us,' whispered Liv.

'They might be in a gang,' added Riley.

'What happened is,' said Liv, still whispering, 'this girl asked where to buy weed. She and her boyfriend wanted to buy $180 worth. So I texted Marco, and he told me to give them his number and say his name was Bob Jones. So, I did, and he comes over, says, "Yeah, I'm Bob Jones, I can get you exactly that much." So they hand over the money, and he says, "Oh, I'll just go get the weed from my place, it's five minutes."'

'Seriously?'

'Yes, and then he fucks off and texts me, "Tell them you gotta go home." So, then this girl—she's coming around here with her boyfriend. Look.' She showed me the text: *My boyf is NOT happi, coming over to urs to wait for Bob.*

'So please can you help us?' said Liv. 'She doesn't know you. Just tell them you haven't seen us, and you know nothing about it.'

I sighed and rolled my eyes. 'Okay, okay. I will help you to deviously *not* sell weed. No biggie.' But I was pleased. This was a sign of a whole new elaborate and exciting life finally materialising before me, a life of coolly facing off criminals and, one day, hacking government databases and parachuting into foreign countries.

Before long, a girl with fried yellow hair was at the door. Two bulky guys were standing behind her, real life 'Crabbe and Goyle' henchmen.

'We're looking for Bob Jones,' she said. 'Is he here, or Liv?'

'No,' I said, 'no one's here right now.'

'Well, we're really pissed off,' she said. She explained the situation, as if leaving a bad review on Trade Me.

'I'm so sorry,' I said. 'I don't know anything about that.'

'Do you know when Liv will be back?' she asked.

'No,' I said, apologetically.

'Dude, let's wait till she gets back,' said one of the henchmen.

'We're going to wait outside until she gets back,' the girl repeated.

'Okay,' I said, and they left to stand by their modified Toyota, where they waited for a few hours, scowling and doing their best to look intimidating. Liv and Riley stayed at the foot of Liv's bed with the lights off, watching *Adventure Time*, the colours moving swiftly over their faces in the dark.

The next day, when Marco came around he was a cocky little shit.

'You know,' he said, 'it's their own fault for trusting a dude named Bob Jones.'

*

'Hey, Maddy,' said Marco, 'I'll give you this bud if you do a mish down to the two-four.'

There were a lot of people I didn't know in the house, crouched on the floor like a flock of birds come to roost for the night.

'That's one good bud,' said a guy whose name I had forgotten, admiring the little palm-sized branch.

'Yeah, that's like twenty dollars right there,' said Marco. 'Look at all those fine-as crystals.'

I couldn't see what they were talking about, but that little bud, like a witch's talisman with its invisible crystals, appealed to me.

'Okay,' I said. 'What are you ordering?' And I was on my way, a real adventurer sliding over the black ice, and the fuzzy white ice. Breath poured out of my mouth like smoke. I was invisible, gliding unafraid under the motorway bridge; the trucks driving close to my skin with their exhaust, gliding over the river which sucked itself down into the dark. I wanted an ice cream.

I returned with my arms full of chips, fried chicken, ice cream and lollies and change. Marco gave me the little bag with the bud, thick with its hidden crystal wealth. I hid it in my bedside drawer and went to bed.

*

There was a boy in my room. He had a sort of army buzzcut and army muscles, but I didn't think he was in the army. He was in high school, or he sold weed at high school.

The boy was lying on the floor with a blanket and pillow. I couldn't sleep with him being there. I rolled over so that my arm dangled off the side of my bed and tried to be as relaxed as I looked. But the room was static, pulled tight, fizzing.

Something wet was on my finger. He was kissing my finger. I saw the dark shape of him. He had moved in close beside my bed. The sensorial shock of being touched in the dark by a warm mammalian other trickled up my arm. I thought maybe it was the way a Victorian lady would feel when she held hands without gloves on for the first time. Maybe it was more like peripheral neuropathy—nerves tingling and deadening, the beginning of paralysis.

I decided, with nothing much to compare it to, that this sensation must be what they called attraction; and that, after this, behaviour would be instinctual. It felt like a movie based on a book based on a story that was read to me as a child.

'Do you want to . . . ?'

I knew the words despite never having been cast in this part before. And I had said I wanted to burn a couch, and I was very aware that I hadn't done it yet; my attempt at an adventurous first year of university was becoming more like a funeral for someone who hadn't even died.

Only, after the word 'yes', the script ended. That was where the scene cut. The sensation was gone and didn't return. I knew it wasn't supposed to be like this, and I didn't want to continue, but all the words had disappeared.

Pain is a simple thing to deal with at the time. I looked at the wall, and there was a little tear in the wallpaper where a staple had been ripped out, and a darker blood red wallpaper was showing through underneath the cream in a jagged star shape, a blemish. I stared at that little blemish and I tried to remember his name.

Brief Intervention

The town square had a morning glow like a cheap tan. The music of last night was circling me. I was still floating as I bought my coffee and as I leaned against the bright supermarket wall waiting for Amber. When she arrived, I climbed into the taxi, feeling as though I had just tucked in my wings and swooped down, landing unsteadily.

'Are you ready?' said Amber in her Canadian drawl. Her long yellow hair was tied in a hasty bun. She had a round face that always seemed beleaguered, eyes ready to chew up pain like a sad old dog.

'No,' I said. 'You?'

'No. No way,' said Amber, and then we were silent. I liked exams. The build-up, the slow sizzling and crackling of nerves, the clean feeling of knowing exactly where you were going, that there were only two possible outcomes and that there was nothing in the world to worry about, finally, except the event itself. Very few activities provided that space for singularity, besides murder–suicides. We were in it together. In fact, though, this exam was voluntary. We had done a three-day training programme, one of the only practical components of our internships, and I had signed up for the exam afterwards with the idea of getting something solid out of my internship, a certificate with a reference, to prove that I'd been here and that I'd gotten something out of the two months in South Africa I'd spent my savings on. *This is to certify*, it would say, *that Madison Ruth Hamill is proficient at providing brief-intervention rehabilitation therapy for substance abuse and dependence.*

Driving through Cape Town was a messy business with everyone going too fast, honking, and weaving in and out of lanes and up onto the footpaths. Fruit-sellers waited at the red lights to knock on car windows, hoping to sell bags of bruised mangoes. Cape Town smelled of sweat mixed into the tarseal, of roadside braai smoke and piss gone stagnant, like the floor of an emptied moshpit.

This driver was not such a bad driver.

'Too fast,' Amber muttered. She said, louder, 'Sir, do you mind going a bit slower?' She always called people sir or ma'am. I couldn't tell if the driver had heard her or was pretending not to have, but he did slow as we approached a line of cars waiting at an intersection, and as he slowed a car pulled out of a driveway to our left, bolting into the back of our left side— my side. I don't remember the sound, just the feeling of my insides being yanked sharply.

The driver must have pulled over then. I don't remember if he cursed and swerved or simply glanced in his mirror and glided smoothly into a space at the side of the road.

'Oh my God,' said Amber and looked at me. She was crying. 'Are you okay?' she said.

I nodded. For a moment I wasn't sure why she was asking me, since she was the one who was crying.

'Are you sure? It was on your side, I think it hit the wheel,' she said.

The driver got out and walked around to inspect the wheel. I opened my door and leaned out. The wheel was wrecked and hubcapless, just a piece of torn rubber around a metal rim. I started to feel lightheaded.

'Yeah, the wheel is fucked,' I said, turning back to sit inside again because I felt too sick to lean out anymore. I could feel the hangover boxing me in. 'Are you okay?' I said.

She nodded. 'It's just the shock. Are you sure you're fine?'

The driver came back to tell us he had called us another taxi. Soon, an identical car arrived, and we were on our way again.

I felt my stomach contract, and I tried to narrow my vision to the powerlines passing over the seat in front of me. It was like the jolt had done something to the hangover and it was getting worse. Amber was saying to the new driver, 'I can't believe ...' and he was saying, 'An older man apparently, shouldn't have been driving, just pulled out without looking.' And Amber was saying, 'Thank God, thank God it wasn't a half-second earlier,' even though she wasn't religious. I hung on, pulling the powerlines hand over hand in my mind. If we could only get there. If I could only keep my head in this exact position and not move until we were there.

The office was a house just off the business district, with a barred veranda and a little sign tacked above the front entrance that read SANCA—the South African National Council for Alcoholism and Drug Dependence.

We were led into a small office. Everything was polished and wooden—that dark wood they used to panel old houses so that they swallowed all the light. I was grateful for the dark and being able to sit. All of the SANCA offices were old houses, barely renovated. The one where we usually worked had been a children's home and there was still a bath in the bathroom, covered in long yellow stains. This one was probably the same, with a big old bath sulking somewhere in a side room.

In his lilting Afrikaner accent, the examiner explained what would happen. Each of us would have a turn to demonstrate our skills in brief-intervention counselling, with the other acting as a client. We would have only a brief time with the client. In reality, we would probably never see them again, so our goal was not to solve their problems but simply to nudge them towards acknowledging that they had problems, or, if they had already done that, towards committing to an attempt at change.

We knew the rules, we had studied for this; but it was reassuring to hear them stated once more with such certainty, like the introduction to a fairy tale. But I soon found I had stopped processing the words. Too soon, Amber began speaking to me in her gentle therapy voice, the hushed tones of reverence that surround sickness like a gauze. She was giving the expected introductory spiel, something like, 'I want to acknowledge the important step you've taken by coming here and seeking help.' I realised we had begun and it was my role to be the client. This was for the best; I was feeling much more affinity with the role of client.

'And can you tell me a bit about why you are here?' said Amber.

Jittery. Jittery was what drug addicts were, and what I was. Was it the hangover or something else? The words just wanted to drop out of my mouth like stones. 'I am, I . . .' I had forgotten who I was meant to be.

'I'm here for my children,' I said. I started to put on an accent, then changed my mind. Two children, I thought to myself, entering high school, the kind that would hate their alcoholic mother. 'I'm worried I'll lose them,' I said, 'and they'll go live with their dad. They hate me.'

'What makes you think they hate you?' asked Amber.

'They said so,' I said. 'I'm a drunk. But I'm worried if I get sober they'll still hate me and then I might as well keep on being drunk.' I was making it complicated for her, but I couldn't stop. 'I couldn't stand seeing them hate me and having to be sober you know?' I said.

Amber paused. 'So, it seems like you're saying you're worried you won't be up to dealing with the problems, when you are sober, that you're used to dealing with through alcohol?'

She was doing very well. I avoided her sad dog eyes, not even because I was in character but because I felt as if I were coming at the world on an angle. I felt myself grow pale and flimsy.

After she was done, the examiner wrote some notes. The sun came in through the blinds and caught the edge of his white hair, giving him a little halo.

'Are you ready?' They were looking at me. In the distance, someone in their car was leaving their hand on the horn.

I nodded. 'Yes,' I said, clearing my throat. One of my legs

had started to shake. I shifted my weight until it stopped, but I felt that the shake had shifted inward.

'Welcome,' I said. My voice, to my surprise, did not shake. 'Thanks so much for coming in. I know it can be quite'—I went blank as copy-paper and couldn't make the word out of the pictures in my mind—'nerve, nerve-wracking,' I said finally, 'to come into this sort of situation for the first time.' I should have been doing the therapist gaze. I had done it so well last week at the course, eyes wide and milky, engaging the client without judgement, and the voice, the soft low voice, like talking to a lover late at night. She looked at me with her dog eyes. She was saying something. She was saying something, and I was nodding, and then she said, 'I want to get better, but I don't know how. What can I do?'

A car was backfiring somewhere far off, or a gun. I said something affirmative about 'acknowledging the problem' but the words felt uncomfortable in my mouth, wouldn't form into sentences easily. The smooth phrases they had taught me to pour like warm water around the anxious mind of the client wouldn't materialise.

Afterwards, as we walked to the train station, my leg began to ache and then the entire left side of my body, the way a bruise grows on an apple. Under my skin I was all dead mush.

'I really want to get home,' said Amber, to my surprise, voicing my own thoughts. 'I think the crash did something to me. I feel kind of sick.'

I tried to match her pace, but I felt as though my legs were tree trunks. I was becoming an Ent, my organs a stiff and creaky nest.

'My leg's sore,' I said.

'Actually,' said Amber, 'should we just get one of the minivan taxies?' She had stopped at a car park where a row of white vans were collecting passengers. 'I don't want to wait for the train.'

I nodded.

'iKapa, iKapa,' a man was yelling.

'Excuse me, sir,' said Amber, 'can you drop us off near Obs?'

He nodded. 'Observatory.' He said something else in Xhosa or Zulu. 'Yes, yes, near hospital.' He motioned to us to get in.

The taxi van was packed but not unbearably so, and we were offered seats. Last time I had been forced to stand, my back bent into the curve of the window, trying not to breathe in an old man's hair, because they had decided to pack twenty-five people into the ten-seater.

'I don't feel well at all,' said Amber.

'Neither,' I said. 'I think I failed the exam.'

'I think I did too.'

'You were fine,' I said.

'Well, we did the exam and we didn't have to,' she said. 'That's the most important thing. At least we made the most of the opportunity.'

The guy hanging out the front door had jumped off at the corner to holler for new passengers: 'iKapa, Cape Town!'

The other passengers were staring into their laps or their phones, their faces glistening. For a moment I pretended that Amber and I were just like everyone else there, tired and on our way home, but they knew from our whiteness and the loose dress-pants we wore because we couldn't handle the heat that we were not, that our time here would end before we could understand it.

'Are you going to the trampoline park?' I asked, remembering the excursion that was planned for us in a few hours.

'No way,' said Amber. 'I'm going home.'

But as soon as I returned to the flat I felt I couldn't stay there alone while all my roommates headed out into the world again, with their shorts on and their cameras ready. They were also foreign interns, from Europe or America, no doubt with a better disposition for their various specialities of social work or occupational therapy. They had the same cheerful openness as they prepared for the next adventure. The black leather couches were hunched under the cool white wall in our living room, but I couldn't sit down. The bruise in my body felt like a violation, as if in the crash something had grabbed hold of my left side and slowly lodged itself in my chest. I couldn't retreat into safety, knowing that it was still there, so I followed them to the trampoline park.

The diving boards reverberated as children jumped into pools of foam cubes. I wanted to bury myself in the foam cubes. I felt as though my bones had been vitrified into delicate china pieces. But it was paid for already, and I had never been to a trampoline park before, and they were giving us free socks— bright mango-orange-coloured ones with pink grippy pads. I had to make the most of it.

I stayed until all my friends were tired of jumping and then I stepped out into the rain, walking my new socks into a puddle, thinking to drown them against their will, and a man being pushed very fast in an office chair down the sidewalk collided with my shins and I had to stumble out of the way.

The next day I wandered around the bright pastel houses of Bo-Kaap until the colours gave me a headache. I threw a braai that night and danced in our yard, making the most of the space we had there, shouting over the barbed-wire fence at the men wolf-whistling, and one of my roommates grew sour in his drunkenness; some old anger I hadn't seen before moved in behind his eyes and he threw a bottle across the road so that it smashed against the church wall, anointing the bricks with beer.

I was running out of time in South Africa and I had to make the most of it. The next day I went skydiving.

Ethnography of a Ranfurly Man

None of us had heard of Ranfurly Draught before we met our flatmate Darren.

'Are you sure other people buy this stuff besides you?'

'Yeah, it's legit,' he insisted. 'It's even got an ad.' The ad was set at a 'man park', a sanctuary of Central Otago grasslands where 'real men', made endangered by such phenomena as veganism and vampire-based romance, roamed freely. The head keeper of Ranfurly Man Park was a blond woman in tight-fitting khaki. She looked through her binoculars as the silhouette of a man reared up on a stallion, the same silhouette that was featured on every can of Ranfurly draught beer.

'They're so'—she paused, turning away to address her audience—'graceful.' As soon as she turned away, the man fell headfirst onto his horse, groaning. Oh, men, we were supposed to laugh. How clumsy, how charming and relatable their attempts to imitate the Ranfurly man, that staunch silhouette, galloping, alone and in control. Any man could join this pursuit, buying Ranfurly Draught and retreating into their secret wildernesses, where we woman would never venture with our unfunny vegan feelings.

'Yeah, it does look legit,' I admitted.

Darren only drank Ranfurly Draught. Only in the large 440ml cans, and only at room temperature. He stacked the empty ones in pyramids near the glass door and we would find them in the morning, pointing towards the sky, the sun glinting off their peaks like a passage to the afterlife. But we couldn't understand his taste. Ranfurly Draught, receiving one or two stars on most beer review sites, tasted more or less the same as the aluminium can that contained it.

Aluminium can be recycled continuously. Theoretically, one Ranfurly Draught can, thrown in the recycling bin, could become a brand new Ranfurly Draught can and reappear on a shelf in a matter of sixty days. In the biblical ways of mass production, multitudes may be fed from the one vessel. Still, I can only guess that one morning, as he gazed in sober contemplation at the pyramid of beer cans before him, Darren decided that he wanted more out of his drinking habit. In the manner of a true Ranfurly Man, he began to build a suit of armour out of his cans.

Darren was training to be a surgeon. Born and bred in Gore, he was never one for chit-chat so he knew he didn't want to become a GP. He was thrilled by the delicate handling of small needles, by the tiniest incisions. He'd stick needles into his own arms for practice. In his room after he came home, he sat and stitched beer cans, piece by piece, tiny incisions, tiny stitches. First the helmet, then the suit. The pull tabs on the lids, he wove into chain mail.

Darren's room was a dense nest woven from the debris of his past experiments. I'd seen it only twice. The first time, I had locked myself out of the flat and, in desperation, prised open his window. I limboed and tiptoed my way through a dense tangle of objects, scraping against them in the dark, though when I thought back on it later, I wondered how it could have been so dark at mid-morning. The second time I was in Darren's room was late one night after we had been drinking. He allowed us all to come in and see the suit of armour glinting on a hook above his bed, the proud red cans with the Ranfurly silhouette in rows along the arms and chest. He took it off the hook and allowed us, one by one, to try on the heavy chainmail and the helmet. With the suit on, I could barely move—my breath enclosed in the metal skull, and the cold rings, like the scales of a fish, against my skin.

'Look how shiny I am!' I said.

'That's enough,' he said, after a few seconds, and he took it back and closed the door.

*

In 1989, a sociologist named Hugh Campbell ventured into a rural Canterbury hotel pub in a town I strongly suspect of being my hometown and began to carry out field work. In this hotel, the local men dominated the public bar, while women and outsiders could drink in the lounge bar. One of the first things Campbell noticed in the public bar was an erect glass phallus. Perched above the bar, for Campbell it was almost too apt a symbol of masculine performance, epitomising both its transparency—'men were scrutinized intensely, and their performance was dissected, during after-work drinking,' he later wrote—and its 'invisibility', whereby the masculine ideal was never spoken about, only displayed. Each day after work, these men would gather beneath the glass phallus, going home later each night for dinner. There was an unspoken agreement among them to act as if they had no wives or domestic responsibilities, and this meant delaying their return home. 'Remember old Metty,' they would say, 'whose wife turned up at the pub and laid his dinner on the bar in front of him . . .' Metty had turned to his wife and demanded, 'Where's my pudding?'

Darren, on the other hand, was a responsible flatmate. Once a week, he spent his afternoon making a roast dinner for the flat. Sometimes he was sent mystery meat from his family back in Gore—kunekune pig or alpaca. More often we would have mutton or chicken or beef. He slow-roasted the potatoes in their gravy till they tasted like chicken all the way through but maintained peak crispiness on the outside. It was a fine art. He served the roast the same way each week, with a small jug of beans on one side and a jug of gravy on the other. Sometimes, when our other flatmates were out late, it was only the two of us at dinner. Darren didn't speak much unless he was drunk or there was medical knowledge that needed explaining. We ate in silence, avoiding eye contact. For a long while I couldn't decide if it was a comfortable silence or an awkward one. But I soon realised that my anxiety was not shared and allowed myself back into the comfortable swell of my own preoccupations. Afterwards we would do the dishes.

'Thanks for dinner,' I would say—the customary post-dinner phrase of our flat—and then we would retreat into our rooms. When I tried to imagine his thoughts I always fell short. I could imagine him performing surgeries in his mind or returning mentally to his home farm, romantically skinning a rabbit maybe, or shooting ducks to get to sleep.

Before Campbell, few scholars had attempted to 'demystify' the rural pub, which was for the most part accepted uncritically, he argued, as 'part of the functioning structure of rural society'. Rural life is often given the mythic qualities of a 'nostalgic fiction of yesteryear', Campbell wrote, contemplating the fairy tales he aimed to dismantle, 'with the rural pub being the centre of this "rural idyll", a retreat from the brutalities of urban living'.

As I saw it, the brutalities of urban living were manifold: the brutality of change, whereby buildings and identities could be wrenched apart and reinvented; the brutality of closeness, of being able to hear one another's shufflings in private spaces, the drunken shouting of State Highway 1 in the early hours, with students returning to the valley in packs, the trucks shaking us in our beds with the strength of moderate earthquakes. Was Darren boxed into that nest of his own making, dreaming of yesteryears?

Below the glass phallus, the men's voices boomed across each other and across Campbell. They raised their eyes from their pint glasses, unfolded their shoulders, unfolded their larger selves. They had known this place for many years.

I can imagine Darren in that pub, in an alternate reality in which he hadn't left home to attend university. In my mind they have his Ranfurly on tap, and he drinks it by the pint, saying, 'Remember old Metty? "Where's my pudding?" Classic.' And then he goes home and cooks his own roast dinner and eats it just the same out of the freezer for a month.

When we drank together as a flat, we played cards and board games. Mostly poker and Settlers of Catan, a game where resources like wool, lumber and ore could be exchanged for roads and houses and quaint seaside churches. We played until we were too drunk to remember the rules. Darren always knew the rules. If he was too drunk to remember the exact details, he'd launch into an explanation all the same.

'No, see here, Maddy,' he'd say in his monotone, 'you can't run an economy with sheep these days, it's all about the ore. You've gotta have the ore.'

Underneath the glass phallus, facts were wielded like swords. Campbell mentioned the cottage he was staying in and a battle ensued, with each man rushing to establish his superior knowledge of the cottage's ownership and history. Another man mentioned seeing a woman driving a truck in a vague location several miles away. The women was quickly identified by the group as an exchange student living with a friend in town, and the relevant nationality-specific jokes were made about her sexuality.

One of the keys to successfully performing masculinity in this pub, Campbell wrote, was claiming 'a legitimate understanding of important local activities such as business, farming, sport, politics, and other local interests'. Just as important was the ability to 'hold your piss', which meant both to handle your alcohol and to suppress the need to pee. The ability to drink the most beer while appearing sober was a highly prized skill built through years of practice.

The first time we played cards as a flat, I stood up to go to the bathroom.

'No, Maddy,' said Darren. 'Don't break the waters.'

'Huh?' I said. It was one of the first conversations we'd had one on one.

'Once you break the waters, you won't be able to stop. Gotta hold your piss, Maddy.' But very soon he contradicted himself and lurched off to the bathroom.

'He has the bladder of an old lady,' another flatmate explained.

Darren had many health problems. As well as bladder problems, he had cirrhosis of the liver. He showed me once, pinching the skin below his ribcage: 'Do you want to feel my liver?' He had night sweats and anxiety, he said, but he didn't explain more except to say that he had taken too many drugs.

Darren socialised mainly with his flatmates and a classmate or two, and through online games. He didn't have a grand social life. He didn't have a romantic partner. I ticked off a list in my head: singular interests, avoidance of eye contact, a tendency to isolate himself, a monotone voice. In a naïve attempt to put a familiar label on him, I asked if he'd considered whether he was on the autism spectrum.

'Nah,' he said, 'I'm not any of that.' I began to suspect his primary pathology was being from Gore.

In his room, glinting like a deep-sea creature, the suit of armour remained. He had never articulated ambitions to display the suit anywhere. He had no particular interest in recycling or wearable arts. He was in the process of building a shield.

The Wilderness

It was grim in the olden days. Humanity was stuck in the wilderness with no electricity, as if, on some uncomfortable tramping trip 'out of Africa' one day, we had stopped somewhere for a long time under someone else's instructions, not knowing when we might move on, when we might finally arrive at the endpoint of human progress. We gave birth to many children in unsanitary conditions, built walls out of skin, slowly learned to disguise our human forms with increasingly fancy manipulations of the flora and fauna—it was important to look good when we finally arrived—and waited year after year for the signal to move on. We built larger and more complex tents for ourselves, with no internet, no reception, but praying, as if holding imaginary cellphones in the air, waiting for reception from the Holy Ghost. People were born and died without internet. They died unable to even google their own names.

In the olden days the danger was in the trees, which wrestled in the hot wind, thick and muscular and full of hiding places. The danger was in the sea, which gnashed at the edges of the forest at all hours without concern. The danger was in each other too. We were restless and wanted to hit each other so badly that we dreamed about hitting each other, and of being hit. We grew tough hides and our teeth dropped out and we didn't care. We died with passion and filth.

Ah, the olden days, the girl sighed, sinking herself further into her duvet. She wished she could travel back in time. The internet heard her sighs and tried to provide her with stories of people riding fast on horseback and chopping each other's heads off and chasing forbidden love. Most things were forbidden back then. It was a simpler time and they would forbid anything just to make it taste sweeter.

The more she read these stories, the more she wanted to run away to the wilderness. But where would she go to find it, now that all this stuff had been built up around her? There was so much safety now that safety had become the main danger, swamping the other dangers, like a monoculture of tall pines suffocating the wild stinging nettles in beds of soft needles. So soft, so tiring. And the little needles whispered to her, 'Lazy stupid failure bitch lazy stupid failure.'

The laptop screen stung and no longer went away when she closed her eyes. The afterglow was a blue bruise. She tried to remember the stories the internet had given her, but she had forgotten them already. They had been good stories that made her brain fill and refill with wonder so that she forgot her body.

For the duration of each story, the pine needles went silent. Without the whispered reminders, she could forget where she was, both literally and figuratively. The internet was magical. She imagined it somewhere in a cloud floating above the Pacific Ocean, sending waves into space and back down into every laptop in the world in thin rainbow bands. She untangled her sheets with her feet and pressed her forehead into the pillow, trying to rest her eyes for a minute.

Lazy stupid failure lazy, lazy stupid bitch failure. It was tiring listening to these whispers. Her friends and acquaintances were moving away and this felt like the slow expansion of the universe. Everything was becoming distant with time, and beautiful from a distance. She imagined her friends being happy, enjoying the conveniences of the post-modern world. They didn't hear these whispering needles, which were only a metaphor and therefore only in her brain because she was a lazy stupid failure.

She let the internet take her away each night until she had to sleep all day, with teenage vampires wandering moodily through her dreams. The internet held her by the eyes and said, 'Don't worry. Don't think about how bad and anxious and lazy stupid failure you are and how everyone despises you secretly. Don't think, don't think about all that.' It provided her with stories about a girl with half a face, about a boy with no limbs, only a head and neck, about a girl turning into a statue, about a war where everyone was gassed so their lungs bubbled, about a heroic mission to save a tortoise with a diseased shell, about a baker who could make a cake look like a designer handbag, about a girl who could make a handbag look like a cake, about a lovely person who was finally truly happy with a rooftop pool, and wanted to share the secret of true happiness in three instalments for only $49.99.

One night she wrenched her headphones off and felt her ears ring like bells. She sat up. Her laptop snapped shut. The next morning, she decided, she would begin her life and not even think about the internet. The internet would become no more than a helpful tool. She would use it the way people in ads for Apple computers used it: while wearing a business suit at a desk, or sharing an astounding joke at a party, or smiling at their children on Skype. She would use it from time to time to ask questions like 'Why am I here?' and 'What should I do next?' and to communicate with her friends and relatives. The internet would become a side note in the margins of her full and productive life.

The next morning she left her phone in its charger, changed from her pyjamas to her togs, and wandered outside and down to the sea. It was grey and purple with yellow silt flooding back out to the horizon. One wave surged again and again onto the sand, chewing hungrily.

She stood staring at the one wave for a long while, nervous that the people who lived on the hills might see her from their windows and wonder why she was swimming alone on an empty beach on a weekday morning. Didn't she have friends? Didn't she have a job? She waded in, pulled on her goggles, and when the water reached her waist she dived under.

Tentacles were close to her skin, pale filmy white tentacles that flailed from bulbous bodies and reached around her; they were translucent with blue spots that were not eyes—jellyfish had no eyes, so they could not be looking at her. She kicked herself upright. She could almost feel their electrical caresses. She pushed back out of the water and onto the sand again. It had been so close, the danger, the danger from the wilderness, just like in the olden days. She ran back to her towel, which she wore like a Roman general. Later, she told her flatmates in the kitchen and they were jealous, she could tell.

The internet was nagging for her to come back with its specials at underwear boutiques and its olden-day documentaries, but it was a trick.

The next morning she put on her togs again. As she walked down the hill without her phone, the shadows of clouds moved south along the ocean floor like stingrays. Jellyfish were dead on the beach and beginning to stink, but the sea looked as clean as a commercial for Hawai'i and only a few loose tentacles floated about, like confetti after a party.

The first wave seethed, saying *fish fish fish*. She walked right in, goggles on, and dived. She kicked and spluttered her way to the old pontoon, where she climbed onto the warm metal and looked out. There was a little flick in the wind-battered surface, a lip which kicked. The dark side of a wave flashed darkly and it could have been a shark. There was no way to tell except to go in, so she dived into the shark-infested water and swam, kicking harder than she had ever kicked, breathing in quick rapturous breaths and kicking up the water so that the sharks might be blinded.

Again, although her legs felt weak, she strode regally in her towel past the early morning dads watching their kids on the slides at the playground. She walked like a hero walking away from an explosion. At home she told her flatmates that she had swum all the way to the pontoon and back, and they were jealous, she could tell.

Her limbs ached as she sat at the kitchen table looking out at the shining sea. The sky was like a child's drawing of the sky.

The wind through the open window ruffled her wet hair. If only it was like this every day, the internet would never win.

The next day she was late heading down to the beach. People were standing all along the roadside and at the end of the wharf, pointing with their phones, so she looked too. She saw them—crescent-shaped appearances, dark big splashes. Dolphins. She had seen dolphins! And with her own eyes, not even with a phone like everyone else. She waded in, and, comforted that there were others already in the water, put her head down and swam towards the pontoon. The water was clear enough to see far down, and she could see the big black anchor going down from the base of the pontoon. She hoped that one of the dolphins would swim up to greet her. She made it to the pontoon, and then she was the closest to the dolphins of anybody. Even then they looked no bigger than splashes. You could tell that if you were taking a picture it wouldn't be very impressive to anyone who had seen even a stock image of a dolphin. But still, it mattered.

Another swimmer arrived at the pontoon and plonked herself down. 'Hello,' the swimmer said. 'They're quite something, aren't they.'

She agreed they were.

That night the rain began and didn't stop and the wind blew at 100 kilometres an hour from the south. She couldn't go to the beach for three days. The internet spoke to her through her laptop screen like God talking through the burning bush. It said, 'Why don't you snuggle down and watch this six-season exploration of vampire–human romance in South Korea, and listen to this collection of soothing thunder sounds, and read this story about this girl who is very happy even though her legs are fused together.'

For a while she disappeared.

She didn't even notice that the storm had stopped until the final season of the Korean vampire romance series had ended. Then she threw her laptop across the bed, having no idea if it had been a day or a hundred years. She walked quickly down to the sea, but the sand had been replaced by jellyfish, ghostly ones, and blue spotted ones and big gloopy pink ones like diseased breasts. The sea crashed furiously against the jellyfish bank. With each flick of wave or seafoam, she watched for a dark spot or a crescent-shaped curve. She thought about dipping a foot in, but the water had become a grey soup of tentacles and sand, and she stood looking out across the wilderness expectantly, as if waiting for the next episode to load.

Author's Note

This book is a work of nonfiction. Everything that happens is true to memory. Times and places have moved around, conversations have been reimagined, and some names have been changed.

Also, some of it is not true, such as the bit about the woman walking around with an axe in her head, and the bit where the internet starts talking. I made that up because sometimes telling the truth requires lying.

Select Bibliography

The Participant

Blanchard, Caroline D., Robert J. Blanchard and R.J. Rodgers. 'Pharmacological and Neural Control of Anti-Predator Defense in the Rat'. *Aggressive Behavior* 16, no. 3–4 (1990): 165–75.

Diagnostic and Statistical Manual of Mental Disorders. 5th ed. Washington, D.C.: American Psychiatric Association, 2013.

Epstein, Robert, Robert P. Lanza and B.F. Skinner. 'Symbolic Communication Between Two Pigeons (Columba livia domestica)'. *Science* 207, no. 4430 (Feb. 1980): 543–45.

Hayhurst, Jill, John A. Hunter, Sarah Kafka and Mike Boyes. 'Enhancing Resilience in Youth through a 10-day Developmental Voyage'. *Journal of Adventure Education & Outdoor Learning* 15, no. 1 (June 2013): 40–52.

McNaughton, N. *PSYC317 Biopsychology.* PowerPoint slides. University of Otago, 2015.

Watanabe, Shigeru, Junko Sakamoto and Masumi Wakita. 'Pigeons' Discrimination of Paintings by Monet and Picasso'. *Journal of the Experimental Analysis of Behavior* 63, no. 2 (1995): 165–74.

Adventure Time

Asch, Solomon E. 'Studies of Independence and Conformity: I. A Minority of One Against a Unanimous Majority'. *Psychological Monographs: General and Applied* 70, no. 9 (1956): 1–70.

Harmon, Dan. 'Pilot'. *Community*, s.1, ep.1, National Broadcasting Company, 17 Sept. 2009.

Ethnography of a Ranfurly Man

Campbell, Hugh. 'The Glass Phallus: Pub(lic) Masculinity and Drinking in Rural New Zealand'. *Rural Sociology* 65, no. 4 (2000): 562–81.

Savage, Carlos. 'Ranfurly Man Park'. YouTube video, 4 Jul. 2011.

Iceland

Attwood, Tony. 'Foreword'. *Safety Skills for Asperger Women: How to Save a Perfectly Good Female Life* by Liane Holliday Willey (London: Jessica Kingsley, 2012).

Cox, Dena, Anthony D. Cox and George P. Moschis. 'When Consumer Behavior Goes Bad: An Investigation of Adolescent Shoplifting.' *Journal of Consumer Research* 17, no. 2 (1990): 149–59.

Kraut, Robert E. 'Deterrent and Definitional Influences on Shoplifting.' *Social Problems* 23, no. 3 (1976): 358–68.

Ray, Joann. 'Every Twelfth Shopper: Who Shoplifts and Why?' *Social Casework* 68, no. 4 (1987): 234–39.

Russell, Donald H. 'Emotional Aspects of Shoplifting'. *Psychiatric Annals* 3, no. 5 (1973): 77–86.

Sale, Anna (host). 'Why I Steal'. *Death, Sex and Money* (podcast). WNYC Studios, 27 Sept. 2017.

I Will Never Hit on You

Bogaert, Anthony F. 'Asexuality: Prevalence and Associated Factors in a National Probability Sample'. *The Journal of Sex Research* 41, no. 3 (2004): 279–87.

Bogaert, Anthony F. *Understanding Asexuality*. Lanham, MD: Rowman & Littlefield, 2015.

'Brooke Shields Remembers "Asexual" Jackson'. *Otago Daily Times*, 8 July 2009.

Brown, Jax Jackie. 'The Desirable Lesbian Crip'. *ABC News*, 20 Apr. 2015.

Decker, Julie Sondra. *The Invisible Orientation: An Introduction to Asexuality*. New York, NY: Skyhorse Publishing, 2015.

Devinsky, Orrin. 'A Year Without Oliver Sacks'. *The New Yorker*, 19 June 2017.

Greaves, Lara M., Fiona Kate Barlow, Carol H.J. Lee, et al. 'The Diversity and Prevalence of Sexual Orientation Self-Labels in a New Zealand National Sample'. *Archives of Sexual Behavior* 46, no. 5 (2016): 1325–36.

Holden, Madeleine. 'What I Learned from My First Month of Drafting Tinder Bios for Cash'. *The Spinoff*, 21 May 2018.

Hucal, Sarah. 'Inside the World of China's Ultra Rich'. *Al Jazeera*, 12 June 2016.

'Janelle Monae Inspires Spike in Searches for "Pansexual".' *New Zealand Herald*, 1 May 2018.

QueerAsCat. 'QAC 36: What Acephobia & Asexual Erasure Looks Like'. YouTube video, 26 Apr. 2015.

Schwarzbaum, Lisa. 'The Revolution Has Been Televised'. *New York Times*, 19 Mar. 2018.

Suckling, Lee. 'Asexuality: Can a Relationship Without Sex Work?' *Stuff.co.nz*, 28 June 2017.

Thomas, Edwin. 'Invisible and Gang-Raped: Living with Disability in India'. *Cable News Network*, 5 Apr. 2018.

Wellings, Kaye, et al. *Sexual Behaviour in Britain: The National Survey of Sexual Attitudes and Lifestyles*. London: Penguin Books, 1994.

Acknowledgements

This book wouldn't exist without the collaboration and support of many amazing, talented people.

I would like to thank Ashleigh Young, who, as my supervisor and then my editor, has been part of this book's construction from the beginning. *Specimen* would never have become what it is without your perceptive and generous feedback.

A big thanks to the rest of the team at Victoria University Press, particularly Fergus Barrowman, Kirsten McDougall, Therese Lloyd and Craig Gamble. Your impeccable taste and passion were invaluable.

To Hannah Salmon for the gorgeous cover art.

To my MA class from the International Institute of Modern Letters: Susanne Jungersen, Glenda Lewis, Catherine Russ, Anna Rankin, Tim Grgec, Rose Lu, Alie Benge, Charlotte Forrester and our tutor Chris Price. Your generous and compassionate feedback, as well as your ongoing support, was immeasurably helpful.

To those who have taken time out of their lives to read *Specimen* and provide feedback at various stages, in particular to Elizabeth Knox, for her encouraging words, and to Olive Owens and Joanna Cho.

To everyone who appears in this book. Thank you for being in my life and for being so understanding.

Last but not least, thanks to my family, who have been unequivocally supportive throughout the process.

I would also like to acknowledge the publications where some of these pieces have previously appeared: RNZ, *Turbine Kapohau* and *4th Floor Literary Journal*.